D1632615

KISS OF YOUTH

When Judy Grant's car broke down in the country, miles from anywhere, she little imagined that the handsome man who came to her aid was her future employer's husband. Nor, indeed, did Richard Portal realise that the girl he had rescued — and fallen helplessly in love with — was his own wife's cousin. It seems that their love is doomed — until the unexpected happens, offering them a chance for happiness greater than they have ever known . . .

Books by Denise Robins
in the Linford Romance Library:

GYPSY LOVER

DENISE ROBINS

KISS OF YOUTH

Complete and Unabridged

LINFORD
Leicester

First published in Great Britain in 1937

First Linford Edition
published 2009

British Library CIP Data

Robins, Denise, *1897 – 1985.*
    Kiss of youth. - - (Linford romance library)
    1. Love stories.
    2. Large type books.
    I. Title II. Series
    823.9′12–dc22

ISBN 978–1–84782–948–1

Published by
F. A. Thorpe (Publishing)
Anstey, Leicestershire

Set by Words & Graphics Ltd.
Anstey, Leicestershire
Printed and bound in Great Britain by
T. J. International Ltd., Padstow, Cornwall

This book is printed on acid-free paper

'A long, long kiss, a kiss of youth and love.'

—BYRON

1

On a chilly June evening, the shabby 'baby car' splashed its way doggedly through a most unseasonable downpour. As it passed along the narrow road, it left a spattering of mud on the banks and bushes on either side.

The girl at the wheel found it difficult to see clearly through the windscreen, because the automatic wiper was working only in spasms. Every time it stopped she had to put a hand up to set the switch going again.

Anyone looking up at the roof could see a thin line of daylight through a horizontal crack across the hood, where it had been badly folded up. Through this crack a steady trickle of water dripped on to the driver's knees. A broken side screen let in a gust of cold air, and every now and then the wind caught the light car, causing it to swerve slightly.

Judy Grant pulled her mackintosh tightly round her knees to catch the water that dripped from the hood.

'Muggins', she addressed the car, 'no one could say you are at your best under these conditions. Still, so long as you get me to Oxford tonight, I'll forgive you for being so darned uncomfortable!'

Unfortunately 'Muggins' had no intention of getting its young owner to Oxford, or anywhere else, for a minute or so later, without any warning, the engine gave a feeble splutter, then quietly, but finally, petered out.

Judy let out an exasperated 'Damn!', steered the car to the side of the road, and put on the hand-brake with an impatient little tug. Opening the door, she jumped out into the rain.

'Muggins', she addressed the car again by the name which she had christened it on the day it was delivered to her, '*must* you choose a fifth-rate lane like this to back out on me, when we're not likely to meet a soul for hours — to say nothing of the fact that it's pouring cats and dogs and we are still forty miles from Oxford?'

'Muggins' sat there silent and self-satisfied, refusing stubbornly to yield to any treatment.

Judy knew a little about cars, although not much. She lifted the bonnet, removed one of the leads, and laid it against its sparking plug. Then she turned the starting handle. There was not the glimmer of response.

'You little brute!' she said, and replaced the lead. 'I suppose it's the mag. That's done *me*!'

With which comment Judy closed the bonnet viciously, turned her collar up round her ears, pushed her hands into her pockets, and set off down the road in disgust.

As she walked the mud squelched round her shoes, and some of it found a way inside. She was not wearing walking shoes. Soon her feet were soaking.

The road twisted pointlessly this way and that, and there was no dwelling of any kind in sight. How dreary it looked, she thought, growing more depressed every moment. The trees on either side were sodden, and the branches dripped and groaned.

She trudged on wearily, mentally cursing her folly in taking this lonely short-cut instead of sticking to the main road. She must reach a garage some-how, because it was essential that she should be in Oxford tomorrow. She was starting a new job. It wouldn't do to arrive late. If she could only find help, so that she could get to some kind of hotel for the night, she could finish the remaining distance tomorrow morning, because she wasn't due at her job until lunch-time. But at the moment the lane looked as if it was never going to end. Curse 'Muggins' for this breakdown! Judy considered the fact that she might have to walk miles before she could get help. Not a car had passed since she started walking, and the time was passing. It must be nearly seven o'clock.

She was tired, cold, and hungry. The rain beat mercilessly against her face. She had been driving all the afternoon from the North, and had had nothing to eat since an early lunch in Doncaster, at the house of an aunt with whom she had been staying. However, she didn't look like getting a meal yet awhile, she told herself ruefully.

She rounded another bend in the road. There was still no sign of human habitation.

She must have walked nearly three miles when suddenly through the discordant symphony of the storm, there broke a sound extremely welcome to Judy's ears. The hoot-hoot of a car. Round the corner appeared a large and luxurious black-and-silver car.

Judy stood in the middle of the road and waved both arms frantically. The car pulled up and a man leaned out.

'Can I do anything?' asked a very pleasant, cultured voice.

Judy came to the driver's side. She could just discern that he was young, attractive, and alone. The car, Judy told herself ruefully, would have passed her ancient seven-horse-power 'baby' haughtily and without recognition. This was a magnificent car. A Bentley coupé. Judy said:

'I'm terribly sorry to bother you, but I've broken down.'

The young man switched off the engine.

'Bad luck. Where's your car?'

'Two miles back. I've been walking — trying to find a garage.'

'I'd better drive you to one.'

'I don't think they'll be able to do much tonight,' said Judy, 'I think 'Muggins' is past aid.'

The driver of the Bentley looked amused.

'Muggins?'

'My little car. I christened it that. It's about nine years old, poor thing!'

'You don't look much more yourself.'

'I assure you,' said Judy indignantly,

'that I'm quite old enough to have a driving licence, and that I drive more enthusiastically than I walk, and I'm so tired I can hardly stand.'

He peered out at her. Now he could see that she was a young woman of possibly twenty-three or four. Rather slim and boyish, and with a brown healthy face. If she used make-up, the rain had long since washed it away, yet she still managed to look nice, he thought. She was hatless. Her cropped brown hair had formed little damp ringlets about her ears. He said:

'Where are you bound for?'

'Oxford.'

'So am I. What about leaving your 'Muggins' until morning and letting me drive you along?'

She hesitated.

'I've left my suitcase . . . '

'Oh, we'll soon nip back and fetch that.'

'Well, it's awfully kind of you . . . '

'Come on!' he said, and opened the door for her.

She did not know how exhausted she really was until she found herself in the warmth and luxury of that lovely car with a rug over her knees. She felt a bit disloyal about 'Muggins', but it was good to be driven like this in a Bentley, which seemed to move on air and run perfectly.

She wondered who her rescuer could be. He was charming. They exchanged the usual comments about the weather, talked 'cars', found the deserted 'Muggins', transferred Judy's suitcase into the Bentley, and then set forth for Oxford, doing a good seventy down the main road.

But they had only driven a few miles when Judy's companion said:

'Look here — I haven't had any dinner. I've been driving all day — from Scotland — and I don't think I can last out without a drink and some food. Will you join me at the next pub?'

'But of course,' said Judy. 'And how frightfully silly of you not to have told me before. You must be terribly hungry.'

The next 'pub' was a small grey-stone inn, warm and welcoming, and quite deserted, because of the weather.

Judy found herself in an oak-beamed room in front of a peat fire, eating ham and eggs, drinking what seemed the best coffee she had ever tasted; on the most friendly terms with a young man who had been a total stranger less than an hour ago.

Wonderful how an incident like this could help one to lay aside one's ordinary British reserve, Judy thought. She was, as a rule, not a communicative girl, but she found herself talking quite openly to her rescuer. What his name was he had not yet divulged, but now that she saw him in the light, she found him extremely good-looking. Tall, yet slenderly built, very black hair, grey, rather narrow eyes, and that brown, hard look of a man who kept himself fit and led an out-of-door life. At first Judy saw him as a gay and brilliant person full of quick wit, ready answers, and a certain facile charm. But she was observant of human nature, and as time wore on she sensed a restlessness, a discontent, and even a melancholy behind the gay mask. He interested her.

She would not drink with him, but they sat smoking cigarettes, and talking, long after the waiter had cleared away.

'That was a grand meal,' he said. 'I wonder if I've ever enjoyed one more.'

'I know I haven't,' said Judy.

He looked at his wrist-watch. Judy noticed that it was of the latest design. Everything about this young man was very expensive. His well-cut grey flannels, silk shirt, wine-coloured foulard tie, and brown suède shoes. He said:

'Do you know it's nearly half-past nine?'

'Heavens!' she exclaimed and put a hand to her mouth.

He was no less observant of her than she had been of him. Without her coat she appeared to be less boyish than he had thought at first. Wholly feminine, and with a very beautiful figure, he thought, in spite of that cheap coat and skirt. He was curious about her. She was obviously not well off. Badly dressed. But there was something most intriguing in her small tanned face with its bright hazel eyes, and he thought he had never seen a mouth with more sweetness and humour. She was sensitive, too. He liked a woman to be sensitive. When he told her the time just now, the colour had stained her cheeks carnation pink. How prettily her small fingers had flown to her lips. He said:

'Must you get to Oxford tonight?'

'N-no!' she said doubtfully. 'It isn't essential but . . . '

'It certainly isn't for me,' he went on. 'Why don't we stay here the night? It's a hell of a night, and we're still some way from Oxford.'

She considered this. Certainly he was right. The rain was still dashing against the window panes, and it *was* so warm and comfortable in here! If they had bedrooms and it wasn't too expensive for her, it would be nice, but . . .

He saw the doubt in her eyes and leaned across the table and smiled. An engaging smile.

'What's the trouble?'

She found herself explaining her position. She had just left a job — an unattractive one where she had been a typist in a big firm in the City. She liked fresh air and sunshine and the country, and had always had it, until two years ago, when her father, a doctor, had died and left her without money, so that she had to work for her living, in any job she could find. She had saved and saved lately, and, with a little money which she had been left by her mother, had managed to buy 'Muggins' (poor 'Muggins', sitting alone in the wind and rain on that deserted road!) and had taken a week's holiday in Cumberland, driving herself round the Lakes. She had had a glorious time, and spent the last day or two with an aunt in Doncaster on the way back. A bit lonely, perhaps, but one couldn't have everything. Now she was going to take up a new job. She was to do odd jobs, including secretarial work, in a country house near Oxford, belonging to a married cousin. This cousin, a girl of Judy's age, had made a very wealthy marriage, and was hopeless about correspondence and accounts, and having heard that Judy was having a thin time, had suggested that she might try the job for a month.

'My cousin is fond of having a good time. I dare say she doesn't want to be bothered with trifles,' finished Judy. 'So I hope to do everything I can for her. I have to be there by mid-day tomorrow, so if I do stay tonight, I must try somehow to get 'Muggins' towed to a garage and present myself at my new job.'

The young man listened and nodded.

'Well, that's all right. You can easily do that. Now let's see if they've got any rooms.'

They had. And one was a room that Judy could afford.

Another hour passed. At the end of

that hour she was sitting in a big chair before the fire and the young man was sitting beside her. They were talking, talking. Talking like old friends. And Judy was no longer tired or depressed. She was conscious of a queer excitement. This was, after all, rather an adventure. Quite the most exciting thing that had happened on her holiday; or, indeed, in her life. It had been rather a dull, difficult life until now. Nothing glamorous in it. Judy had been growing more and more conscious of the need for glamour in everybody's life. And that was what this very glamorous young man was saying to her.

'I think it's such a crime that a young and lovely girl should drift on in dreary jobs and never do anything exciting,' he was saying. 'I seem to spend my time with women who have so much money they don't know what to do with it, and so much time on their hands that they just become egotistical and selfish and difficult. But you — you've got courage and you're gay without a bean in your pocket, and you've enjoyed this week in your 'Muggins' much more sincerely than the majority of the girls I know would like being driven by a chauffeur down to the South of France.'

'That sounds cynical,' said Judy.

'I think I am cynical,' he said. 'Or was until I met you. But you're being very good for me. Or bad for me, I don't know which.'

Judy blushed violently. He thought her quite lovely when she blushed. He said:

'I haven't met anybody like you for years — if ever. I'm afraid I rather waste my life, too. No work. Too much money and the pursuit of pleasure.'

'It sounds all right to me,' said Judy.

'But you don't mean that. You'd like a man to do something worthwhile, wouldn't you?'

Judy ran her hand through her brown curls, which had long since dried by the fire and had little gold lights in them now.

'Yes, I suppose I would. But you can't *help* having a lot of money.'

'No, but if you had it, you'd do something useful with it, wouldn't you?'

'Why should you think that?'

'I don't know. I just feel you wouldn't chuck it wantonly away. In fact, I think you're *real*. And I'm tired to death of everything artificial and futile. Tell me what you'd do if you were rich.'

They talked earnestly for another half-hour. Then Judy suddenly changed the conversation and said:

'Do you know, we don't even know each other's names?'

He threw away the cigarette which he had finished, and gave her a sudden whimsical look from his handsome eyes.

'I don't think I shall tell you mine. You might recognise it. I'm often to be seen in the *Tatler* and *Sketch*, and there are paragraphs in the papers about my racing car, and my motor-boat, and me at a race meeting and me at a dance, and so on. Just an idle young man of no use in the world. I'm ashamed of it when I talk to you and see what you've got to face up to, and how well you do it. I don't suppose for a moment you want to be a private secretary to a spoiled Society woman, even if she *is* related to you. You'd like a home of your own. Tell me, have you ever been in love?'

The colour stung her cheeks again.

'No,' she said.

'But when you do fall in love — that will be something real to you. It'll *be* love — and that's a thing I'm still looking for, I think.'

'Why are you saying all these things against yourself?'

'I don't quite know.'

'I think you're so awfully nice,' she said with a simplicity which enchanted him.

He leant forward, looking at her earnestly.

'I'm not going to ask your name, since I won't tell you mine. Yes, I will — I'd like to know your Christian name.'

'Judy.'

'That's sweet. Rather old-fashioned. Are you an old-fashioned girl, Judy?'

She was suddenly tongue-tied. She had never met anybody quite like him. He had the gift of words — the gift of making her feel that he was deeply interested in her, which was such subtle flattery! Her heartbeats began to speed a little.

'In what way?' she asked.

'Well — you say you haven't been in love. Have you ever had even a passing affair?'

She laughed self-consciously.

'Ye-es! When my father was alive there was one young man — and one in the office who kissed me the other day, and I thoroughly disliked it on both occasions.'

'And is that all you know of love, Judy?'

'Yes,' she said, and her hands moved a little nervously. 'But, Mr . . . '

'I'm not Mr. anything to you,' he broke in. 'I tell you, I'd rather you didn't know my name. I may never see you again after tonight. I don't suppose I will. But you said that you think me very nice, and I want you to go on thinking that. And if you must call me anything, let it be Dickon, which was my mother's name for me, and nobody else uses it.'

'That's as old-fashioned as Judy.'

'I'm going to have another drink,' he said suddenly. 'Unless everybody in this place is asleep.'

He stood up. How tall he was, she thought. There was something of the old-fashioned 'exquisite' in him. And that mixture of melancholy and insouciance which was so fascinating. He rang the bell, but nobody appeared. It was quiet now outside as well as indoors. The storm had died down.

It struck Judy suddenly that she was very much alone with this young man who asked her to call him 'Dickon', who refused to give his real name, and who presented himself to her as a futile member of society.

Like old friends, they had talked to each other of life and its problems. But she could not help wondering whether she had been wise to come with him — or indeed, wise to stay here tonight like this. She was not afraid of him. He had said and done nothing to give her a mistrust. And she had never been afraid of herself. For the last two years she had been on her own. A practical streak and a sense of humour had pulled her through the various difficulties which a young attractive girl must occasionally face.

For a while she had been more or less content to live her life alone and let work be her aim and object. Recently her loneliness had increased. But she knew, definitely, tonight, after talking to this unknown man, that the essential need in a woman's life was love and a lover. Absurd that a total stranger should make her aware of such a fact. But this Dickon did.

With sudden dread, she remembered tomorrow. She thought of lovely, spoiled Amanda, her cousin, who had unlimited means and lived in one of the historic country homes of Oxfordshire. Amanda wouldn't be easy to live with. It was kind of her, of course, to give Judy the chance of a lovely home. Miles better than slaving away in a City office, living in digs in Ealing. But — as Dickon had said — Judy did not really want to be at anybody's beck and call. She wanted a home of her own. And Amanda changed her mind so often about everything, possibly she would change her mind about this, and send her new secretary and help off at a moment's notice.

Judy felt infinite curiosity about Dickon. Who was he really? Where did he come from? Was he married or single? Somehow she hoped he was not married. Ridiculous! Because she would never see him again!

Dickon set down his empty glass and came close to her.

'Everybody must be asleep. You look tired, little Judy.'

'Perhaps I am a bit now. Perhaps I'll go to bed.'

'No, don't leave me yet,' he said quickly. 'You're doing me so much good. Driving away all kinds of devils in me, Judy. Do you know, I have an insane wish to destroy my expensive car and get out of my expensive life, and just go off in a car like Muggins — with you. And really, sincerely enjoy myself. Would you come — if I asked you to?'

She made no answer. What he suggested was fantastic. Something — she knew not what — caught her by the throat. Suddenly she said:

'I've never met anybody like you in my life — Dickon.'

'God!' he said. 'How sweetly you say that name.'

And before she knew what was happening, he had made a sudden movement, pulled her up into his arms, and set his lips to her mouth.

2

Dr. Hugh Martin had had a very long, tiring day. Having finished his rounds, which had taken up more time than usual, he had immediately been called out on an urgent summons to Checkley, a village thirty miles away from his own home. His cousin, Robert Tardale, had wired that his little girl had been knocked down by a car, that the local doctor had not been able to discover the extent of her injuries, and Tardale had begged Hugh to come at once.

Being a friend of his cousin's, and very fond of the child, Hugh had immediately set forth through the wet, chilly June night for the Checkley Inn, which was run by his cousin.

On his arrival, he had been thankful to find that the child was suffering chiefly from bruises and shock, and that she was not seriously hurt.

Now he sat with Robert Tardale in the saloon bar at the inn, smoking cigarettes and drinking whisky and soda.

'I can't tell you how grateful I am, Hugh,' Tardale was saying. 'I'm sorry you had the trouble of coming along on such a beastly night. This doctor here came in and talked a lot about there being a possibility of Daphne having internal injuries, and I got rather scared. It's a tremendous relief to know there's nothing really serious. If I'd known, I wouldn't have dragged you over here.'

Hugh remarked that it didn't matter, and that he was only too thankful that it was no worse. But at the same time he felt irritated because the local doctor had frightened Robert into sending for him. He well understood how anxious his cousin must have felt, as he was devoted to the child. But there had really been no cause for alarm and no suspicion of internal injuries. Daphne would be up and about again in a week, he told Robert.

Hugh wouldn't stay long talking. It was past eleven now, and before he reached home it would be well past midnight. He had to get back to Oxford.

As he sauntered along the hall in search of his hat and mackintosh, followed by his cousin, he glanced in passing into the lounge, the door of which was half open. He caught a glimpse of a room softly lighted, of a large glowing peat fire, partially hidden by two figures, a man and a girl, who stood, very close together, locked in each other's arms. The girl was small, with brown curly hair and a lovely figure. Pretty, too, thought Hugh Martin. He was attracted by the look of her. He could not see the man so well, but he noticed that he was tall and slenderly built. Hugh was just about to pass on, when something familiar about the man made him pause and look for a moment. Surely he had seen him before. His face was hidden from him, but he was almost certain he recognised that slender, well-dressed figure, and that handsome head with the jet-black hair. Hugh Martin raised his brows, then turned to his cousin.

'Who have you got in there?' he asked, as they continued their way to the front door.

Robert Tardale gave him a knowing look.

'Well, I don't exactly know who they are,' he said. 'But I imagine it's one of those cases where the fewer questions asked the better. They turned up in a marvellous Bentley some hours ago, and booked for the night.'

'It wasn't a black-and-silver car, was it?'

'Yes — how on earth did you know?' said Robert. 'Do you know them?'

'The man's a patient of mine,' the other replied with a slight smile. 'I thought he was a pretty steady kind of fellow, but I suppose one really knows nothing about one's friends' private lives.'

'But who is he? And who's the girl?

Do you know her?'

Hugh was rather vague. After all, it wasn't his business. He told Robert that he didn't know the girl, but that the man lived near Oxford not far from his own house. He refused to give any more information, and murmuring something about 'professional etiquette', he collected his hat and mackintosh in the hall, and bade his cousin goodnight.

Meanwhile the two in the lounge were completely unconscious of anyone but each other.

It seemed to Judy that time itself stood still as Dickon's arms closed about her and his lips drew from hers the first real kiss of passion that she had ever given or received. Nothing, *nothing* like those other kisses she had spoken of, hurriedly snatched, and even objected to. This was different — this sudden mad intoxication, this breathless surrender which made her little world spin dizzily around her, this complete awakening to love, and the annihilation of every other emotion in her heart.

Love! *Love!* This, then, was love, and what madness, indeed, when it was for somebody whom she hardly knew, a young man still a stranger, yet suddenly grown intimate, suddenly become the one and only man in the world who could unloose that wild torrent of feeling and make her say to herself:

'This is *he*. This is my lover. The lover for whom I have been looking. The only one in the whole wide world!'

Oh, that long, long kiss, unforgettable and irrevocable, signing and sealing her his! She was neither afraid of him nor of herself. It seemed the most natural thing in the world to do, to lean against his heart and feel the strong quick beats of it, to put both arms around his neck, to be drawn closer and closer; and finally when he lifted his head, and said:

'Judy, little Judy, do you love me?' she answered:

'Yes!'

And that must be crazy — to say that she loved him, knowing nothing whatsoever about him, and he knowing nothing about her.

But pure instinct led her to ask in her turn:

'Do you love me?'

And he answered with a quiet sincerity which was immensely satisfying to her:

'Yes, Judy. I've fallen in love with you quite hopelessly, my dear.'

But almost as soon as the words left his mouth, there flashed through his mind the memory of another face and of a very poignant reason why he had not the slightest right to tell Judy or any other girl that he loved her.

''Hopelessly' is the word,' he added to himself, and a sudden look of bitter misery replaced the ardour in his handsome eyes. Gently he released Judy. As she stood there, breathless, hazel eyes shining at him, questioning him, he made no effort to take her back into his arms.

She said in a rather shaky voice:

'I suppose I oughtn't to have let you kiss me like that. But I just couldn't help it.'

He found her simplicity very moving.

'How sweet you are,' he said.

'It's absurd, isn't it?'

'Why absurd?'

'Well — a bit crazy, if not absurd.'

'I suppose so. Are you sorry?'

Judy put both hands up to her cheeks. They were flaming. She had never felt so mad, so exalted, so forgetful of everything but this Dickon and that long, ecstatic kiss. He might walk out of her sight and out of her life this very minute, she told herself, but she loved him and always would. She was not a fatalist by nature, but she felt that there was something of fate about this — this meeting with Dickon, and the overpowering impulse which had led them into each other's arms.

'No, I'm not sorry,' she said. 'I couldn't be.'

The misery sped from his eyes again, leaving them full of warmth and tenderness. He felt very grateful towards her for not spoiling this perfect moment. *She* was perfect. Not silly, giggly, ashamed.

But accepting this lightning passion with a fine simplicity, a generosity that in his estimation set her above other women. He adored her for not being sorry about it, nor anxious, nor, indeed, anything but glad.

The warmth and sweetness of her in his arms and the response of her lips had, he fully realised, sprung from the most sincere feeling, and from no light sensuality. Judy could never be light in any way, nor capable of the wiles and common artifices of others of her sex. Nor, for instance, generous with her kisses for ulterior motives, like that other whom he had held and kissed — one who was just a perfect artist with her imperfections and cajoleries.

Once he had thought he had loved that woman, and she had almost broken his heart and his life. And since then he had felt many surface attractions, *en passant*, and played the old game with women who knew the rules as well as he did, caring for nothing, nobody, for long. He believed himself to be a judge of women, nowadays. And he believed implicitly that this girl, Judy, who had come into his life so unexpectedly tonight, would never regard love as a game to be played, and would never wish to play at it. She would love only because it seemed a serious thing in her life. And when she loved, it would be genuine and for ever.

A kind of groan came from him.

'Oh, Judy, Judy!'

'What is it?' she whispered.

He was speechless, torn with a confusion of thoughts, doubts, regrets. Most of all, regrets.

Judy, perplexed, but still on the summit of the glorious emotion which flooded her very being, drew nearer him and looked up at him with her bright hazel eyes. The pupils, he thought, were larger, darker than ever. What lovely luminous, honest eyes they were.

The recklessness and unrestrained longing which had led him first to kiss her, led him now to pull her back into his arms. He covered her warm flushed face with kisses, and with feverish kisses closed her eyelids and brushed her lashes.

'My sweet,' he said, 'there's so much sweetness in you that it almost hurts me. Darling, listen . . . we don't know each other's names, and I've told you less about myself, perhaps, than you've told me about *yourself*. Maybe we were wise. Maybe it would ruin everything if we started to be sane and practical and conventional. Let's go on being crazy like this, my dear — just for a little while.'

'But, Dickon . . . '

'Please,' he interrupted urgently, his lips close to her ear, 'please don't let's spoil things with any questions or explanations now. I love you and I want you to love me. Don't let's remember anything else, Judy. Let's go on dreaming this dream together, in case we wake up and find that it isn't true.'

She was baffled and a little uneasy. What did he mean? Why should it be only a dream? Why need they ever wake up and find it untrue? To her it was so very real. The new-found nearness and dearness of him. All the beauty and romance, the thrill of loving and being loved, which she had not known before and which she realised had been sadly missing from her mundane life.

But if she was dreaming, certainly, she told herself, she had no wish to wake. Neither did she wish to spoil it all by coming down to earth, while this heavenly craziness lasted. If only it *could* last!

Dickon kissed her again, then pulled her down to a big armchair with him, opposite the peat fire which was still red and glowing in the grate.

The glow of it was on her face and in her heart. He thought how marvellous she looked. He kept one arm close about her, and with sensitive fingers traced the tender outline of her beautiful brows and cheeks. As those fingers brushed her lips, she kissed them impulsively, and he felt a rush of love for her such as had never before entered his heart for any other woman. An amazing love, which had no selfishness, no egotism in it, only a deep wish to do homage to her; an aching desire to keep her present trust in him unshaken. Futile hope, he thought wretchedly. Why, in heaven's name, should life have played this trick upon him — brought him so much too late in contact with a personality that might have made such a very different man of him. And why, also, should this unknown slip of a girl, who worked for her living, seem to him like a star shining higher and brighter than any woman in the world?

He lifted one of her hands and looked at it.

'What a little hand, Judy,' he said.

'But it's strong,' she said. '*I'm* very strong.'

'In spite of being so little! Yes — you may look like a kid, Judy, but you're really a very capable young woman, aren't you?'

35

'I don't know, but I've learnt to look after myself.'

He put his cheek against hers.

'You're not looking after yourself too well tonight, sweet. Why do you trust me like this?'

'I just do.'

He trod on the wish to be honest and open with her, just for the sake of prolonging this lovely moment.

'Tell me all the things that you can do, Judy.'

'Nothing very exciting. I can type, and I'm quite good at keeping accounts, and I can cook a bit, and I make my own clothes — but how dull!' She laughed.

'How gifted!' He laughed with her.

'I can drive a car, too,' she reminded him.

'And what a car!'

'Are you being rude about my 'Muggins'?'

'I wouldn't for the world. I shall always think of 'Muggins' with joy. She's a grand little car — grand like the driver.'

'But your Bentley's grander still.'

'Not in the same way. It just stands for speed and wealth, whereas 'Muggins' stands for . . . '

'Poverty and a breakdown,' she finished for him.

'*And* work *and* simplicity, and oh, Judy, how glad I am that 'Muggins' let you down tonight, my dear.'

'I'm glad too,' she whispered.

'Are you looking forward to your new job?'

He tried to speak casually and avoid the temptation of suffocation her with kisses.

'I was — in a way. I hope I shall get on with my cousin and do my job properly, anyhow.'

'You'd do any job properly.'

'You say such lovely things to me, Dickon. But I want you to tell me more about yourself.'

He felt restless and miserable again. His throat was hot and dry. He felt Judy's cool young lips on his forehead. He heard her say:

'Why won't you tell me more about

yourself? Can't you see that tonight has changed everything for me, and I can't think about my job or anything but you now, just *you*, Dickon darling?'

She could have said nothing more calculated to trouble his conscience. He moved away from her deliberately, got up, drew out his cigarette-case and feverishly lit a cigarette. 'This is mad, Judy. Go to bed, my dear. Go along, please.'

She stood up and looked at him with wide, troubled eyes. She could see that something beyond her comprehension was unnerving him. His reluctance to tell her anything about himself filled her with an indefinable uneasiness. She said:

'Do you really want me to go!'

He avoided her eye.

'Yes,' he said. 'We'll meet in the morning. Good night, Judy.'

Her heart sank. The thrilling splendour of this new and wonderful romance seemed suddenly to recede — to vanish out of her reach. But since

Dickon seemed to have no further wish to keep her with him, nothing would have induced her to stay. She walked slowly to the door.

'Good night, Dickon,' she said.

He raised miserable eyes to her, then suddenly sprang to her side and caught her in his arms again. He kissed her wildly until her face, her lips, were burning.

'Good night, darling, *darling*! I love you! Always remember that I love you.'

She wanted to say something in her turn, but the inclination to burst into tears made her speechless. She broke away from him, ran out of the room and somehow found her way up the staircase to her bedroom. 'No 7,' the proprietor had told her.

She switched on the light, and for a moment, panting, white with emotion, looked around her. A typical, rather gloomy country 'pub' bedroom, with its plastered walls, heavy black beams, and bare polished boards. On the bed lay her suitcase, still unopened.

She could not understand why Dickon had so suddenly changed his attitude and sent her from him, or what that last wild embrace had signified. She only knew that she was as unhappy now as she had been happy a few moments ago. The hot tears were welling into her eyes. For a moment she stood still, hesitant, half inclined to run downstairs and insist upon an explanation of his mysterious attitude. Then, suddenly, she heard the unmistakable sound of a big car being started up — of the hum and throb of a big engine in the silence of the night. A sound which she recognised. It was the Bentley, in which she and Dickon had come to the inn.

Surely it was not Dickon going away, leaving her — like this.

She rushed to her window and flung it open. The chill damp air struck against her flushed face. She saw a broad white beam of light and heard the crunch of wheels on the cobblestones in the yard. Straining her gaze, she could just see the long black-and-silver body of a car — Dickon's car — and Dickon at the wheel, guiding the Bentley out of the garage and on to the road.

She cried out frantically, knowing that she would not be heard.

'*Dickon!*'

The car, with exhaust roaring, moved off into the night. The gleam of light vanished as it turned the corner. Stupefied, Judy drew back from the window, realising that Dickon had left the inn, knowing intuitively that he did not mean to come back.

3

Judy walked to the bed and sat down on the edge of it. She was trembling and she felt very cold. And every nerve in her body was jumping. In a dazed way she started to unpin the brooch from the white piqué collar of her dress. And in a dazed way she kept asking herself again and again why Dickon had gone away. Of course he might come back. It might be that he had just gone out in the car for a run. But that was unlikely. He had been driving all day. He wouldn't want to take the car out for pleasure now. It must be the urgency of his own feelings that drove him away. Away from *her*. That was the thought which caught Judy by the throat.

Turning to the bag which still lay unopened on her bed, she lifted the lid. Her chilled, shaking fingers found nightgown, dressing-gown, and slippers, and lifted them out. She undressed, and a few moments later lay rigid between the cold sheets. The curtains were drawn back from the window. Her eyes stared into the darkness. Her ears strained for the sound of a car — for the deep hum of the Bentley returning to the inn.

One hour, two, three went by. But the silence of the night remained unbroken except for an occasional hoot from the mournful throat of an owl in the valley.

The grey misty dawn, damp and melancholy after the storm, broke over the countryside and lightened the oak-beamed bedroom in which Judy lay, still awake. Tired though she was, she had not found refuge from the torment of her thoughts. She only knew that Dickon was not coming back. For some reason or other he had 'run out on her'. Loved her for a few hours, made himself the most thrilling, romantic lover any woman could desire, drawn her very soul through her lips with his kisses, then gone his way.

What was the mystery? Why had he said all those warm, lovely things to her — as warm and lovely as those kisses on her mouth — and then in a furtive, almost cowardly way, rushed out into the night? What had *she* done? Had she made herself cheap? Had he just been amused with her — then afraid that she was too serious — decided to get out as quickly as he could?

That made her whole body burn with shame — for herself and for him. Yet something rebelled against the thought. Something told her that it wasn't true. There was a much deeper mystery behind Dickon's love-making and his abrupt departure.

Her eyes were red-rimmed with fatigue and sleeplessness, and her heart weighed down by depression, when at length she got up, took a cold bath as a much-needed tonic, dressed and went downstairs.

The little country inn seemed strange and unfamiliar in the morning light.

Queer how different a place can look when one arrives at night. And Judy, staring about her with miserable eyes, thought how different she had felt when she had first entered this hotel with Dickon. Why, why had she allowed herself to be caught up in the mad enchantment of those hours with him? She might have known it was a crazy thing to do; that she would suffer for it.

She found a young porter washing down the stone passage, and asked him how long it would be before she could have breakfast. He told her at least an hour. Then she thought of poor 'Muggins' sitting out on the road, miles back. The thought brought her back to earth with a bump. No good sitting in the clouds, sighing about last night. She must put that out of her mind and regard it as a dream. Hadn't he said:

'Let's go on dreaming this dream together, in case we wake up and find that it isn't true!'

He had known *then* that it couldn't be true. But she had been a mad little fool, in a fool's paradise.

On questioning the man, she found that the nearest garage was only a few hundred yards up the road. She decided to walk to it and get them to tow in 'Muggins'. If the car could not be repaired on the spot, she would then have to get to a station and so to Oxford and her job. Amanda was expecting her. And just because she had made an idiot of herself last night, it was no reason why she should start off badly in her new career by arriving late.

The porter dried his hands on a towel, fished in his pocket and brought out an envelope.

'You're Miss J. Grant, aren't you?'

'Yes.'

'Found this on the hall table, miss, and was going to send it up with your early tea.'

Judy came out of the daze in which she had been since she heard Dickon's car drive away from the hotel. The pupils of her eyes dilated as she put a hand out for the envelope. She knew at once it was from *him*. Her pulses thrilled. Perhaps now, at last, she would solve the mystery of last night's affair which had been so brief, so tempestuous, and — so far as she was concerned — so tragic. For she loved Dickon. If she never saw him again, she must go on loving him. She had known that the first moment he took her in his arms. She was shaking as she read the letter. If she had expected a long explanation, she was destined to disappointment. He had only a few lines.

'*Sweet, I can only ask you to forgive me, although I'm too selfish to want you to forget. But I'm married, Judy. That's why I didn't dare stay. That's why we mustn't meet again. I love you. I'll remember you and last night all my life. Good-bye.*

Dickon.'

Judy folded the note up and put it in her bag. She turned from the porter's curious gaze and walked out of the

47

hotel, down the quiet road to the garage. She thought:

'So *that's it*. He was married.'

That was why he had gone. Not because he was afraid for himself, but for her. There were plenty of men who might not have played the game, as Dickon had done. For a while, he had allowed himself to forget his position, as lost as she was in the terrific emotion which had led them into each other's arms. Then he had remembered — and gone away. What else could he do? It was better than seeing her, explaining to her, going through a scene.

Judy walked on blindly. She did not see the countryside because of her scalding tears. They dripped down her cheeks as she walked. She felt broken-hearted. It was so very hard to find your lover and lose him — all in a night. To know that he was married — that he belonged to another woman and that she would never see him again. She knew nothing much more about Dickon now than she had known yesterday. She did not even know his surname, or what his wife was like, or if he was happy. But of course he was unhappy, or he would not have made love to her in that way, she argued with herself. She was certain he wasn't happy.

She tried to remember all the things he had said. Things which made her feel very near to him, even though he was gone. Things which she could go on remembering. After all, he did not want her to forget. He said that. She drew forlorn comfort from that fact. And from his note which she could keep for ever. In it were written the words he had said so many times last night: '*I love you.*' She could read them every day till she died if she wanted to.

Now she was sure that it wasn't just a passing amusement for Dickon. It had been real to him as it was to her. That would be grand comfort in the days ahead which must be empty of love — such love as he had shown her.

As she neared the garage, Judy

dashed the tears from her eyes and lifted a young, determined chin. This was where she must regain sanity and sense, she told herself. She must just look on that episode with Dickon as a lovely miracle — a revelation that she wouldn't have missed for all the world. But it was no good sitting down and crying about it. And one couldn't live on memories alone. There were other things in life. Work. She had always worked. And the thought of Dickon must be locked away in her heart. Nobody would ever know about it. Nobody in the world.

Judy was her cool, practical young self again when, a few hours later, she drove 'Muggins' as fast as it would carry her to Oxford.

The garage had soon put the little car in working order again, and as she rattled along through the miles, Judy looked through the torn side-curtains which flapped in the wind, and her sense of humour stole back; brought some colour into her cheeks and a gleam into her tired eyes.

It really was comic — as well as tragic. Last night Judy Grant, arriving at an hotel in a gorgeous Bentley with a gorgeous young man, dreaming a dream of love with him for a few glamorous hours. And today . . . Judy Grant, driving alone in her little shabby old car, to a new job with only a farewell letter in her bag to prove that it hadn't all been a figment of her imagination.

What *would* the aunt in Yorkshire have said? The *idea*, she would have said! Her niece getting mixed up in such an affair with somebody whose surname she did not even know! Cousin Amanda wasn't so likely to be shocked. She led the free-and-easy life of the smart and wealthy crowd. But she was the last person whom Judy intended to tell.

A very weary Judy arrived before lunch at 'White Monks', which was her cousin's house, just outside Oxford.

Thoroughly disturbed though she

was, emotionally, Judy thrilled with pleasure as she drove through the wrought-iron gateways into the beautiful grounds of what had been a monastery in the days of Mary Tudor. Part of it had been restored at a later period. It was a grand place, built of grey stone and partially timbered.

The sun had just broken through a bank of cloud, and before Judy's rapt vision appeared the green loveliness of trees, perfectly kept parkland, and finally 'White Monks'. The flower gardens were the loveliest Judy had ever seen. There was so much colour everywhere that it almost took her breath away. Acres of roses. And scarlet roses rioting over the grey stone walls of the house. Roses right along the terrace which led down to lawns and tennis courts. Roses tumbling in cascades among the stone archways of the cloisters which had not been altered since the monks occupied the place. And this was the Portals' home.

Lucky Amanda, thought Judy, to live

here. And lucky for her, Judy, to get a job in such a heavenly place. When she had met Amanda in Town and talked things over, Amanda had said that it was 'lousy living in the country' and she much preferred their London flat. Now that she saw 'White Monks', Judy could not understand it.

But there were a lot of things about her cousin Amanda which she did not understand, so she discovered when she sat at lunch with her that day.

The meal, which the two girls had alone on the terrace, was served outside in the sunlit grounds under a striped umbrella — exquisite food served by two menservants in white coats. So much magnificence was a little nerve-racking for Judy, who had led a very simple life. But Amanda Portal took it all for granted. And she appeared both disgruntled and dissatisfied.

'Thank God, you've come, Judy,' she said as they ate their iced melon. 'You'll be able to run the whole place nicely for me, my dear, and manage the staff, which I loathe doing. And Ricky won't have a paid housekeeper because he says they're no good, and he thinks I ought to be the dutiful little wife and run the place for him. But I can't and I won't.'

Judy smiled at her cousin.

'So the impoverished relation is hauled in to do it. Well, I'm only a paid housekeeper, aren't I?'

'No, I can tell Ricky that as you're one of the family, so to speak, you'll cherish the place as though it's your own. He's crazy about 'White Monks', my dear. But I'm bored to tears, and once you've got everything under control, I can go away so much more and Ricky can't grumble.'

'Does he grumble much?'

'Now and again. But I don't take any notice. In fact, we don't take much notice of each other, as you'll find. We aren't really on the best of terms.'

'I'm sorry to hear that.'

'You needn't be. We're used to it. I go my own way as much as I can. We weren't really suited to each other, and I assure you, if I could find anybody with as much money as Ricky, I'd elope speedily!'

Judy felt shocked and looked it. Amanda Portal laughed.

'I can see you're just the same as ever, Judy. Full of ideals and high principles. Well, long may you keep them, my dear. By the way, have you got a nice young man in tow?'

The colour sprang to Judy's face and her lashes fell quickly.

'No.'

Amanda Portal thought:

'What a funny little thing. She actually blushes. It's too deliciously out-of-date. But I rather like her. And I think she'll manage very well. She's very domesticated, and she's quiet and won't get in my way. As for Ricky, I'm sure he'll think she's 'a dear little thing'!'

Judy was thinking:

'I could never possibly tell Amanda about — *Dickon*.'

Amanda did not inspire confidence. She had always been hard as a child, when Judy remembered her. But now, at twenty-two, she was as sophisticated and blasé as a woman of forty. Beautiful — Judy had never seen anybody more attractive physically than Amanda, with her long, lithe body, the rich gold of smooth hair pinned madonna-like into a knot at the nape of her white neck, and queer, narrow, greenish eyes heavily fringed with lashes. She used a lot of make-up. Her mouth was a give-away, Judy thought — that thin scarlet curve had a cruel twist to it, a selfish droop. When Amanda smiled, she was charming. But her face in repose suggested that she could be as hard as nails.

Judy felt inclined to pity Richard Portal. Or perhaps he was just as bad. Perhaps they were both just selfish, spoiled children of fortune.

During the meal, Amanda talked a lot about her various admirers, a new racing car which Ricky was buying her (she had already had a good laugh at the cherished 'Muggins', and called it 'too amusing'); the big dance they were going to hold down here at the end of the month, the difficulty of keeping a staff in a country house, nowadays; and the various domestic duties which would fall upon Judy. The correspondence which she could deal with. Demands for charities, local invitations, etc., etc. Amanda had no time for any of that, she said, and she was always getting into trouble with Ricky for being rude and neglectful of her duties. Now she would get Judy to perform them for her. And it would leave her nice and free.

Luncheon over, Judy was taken through the house. So much magnificence took her breath away. She could only get a confused impression of the many rooms, full of rare furniture, mostly Dutch marquetry which had been collected by Ricky's father; wonderful rugs, rare paintings and china. A room furnished in modern style, with radio-gramophone, and a dance floor — which Amanda called her 'playroom'. And thence upstairs where, so far as Judy could see, the Portals had separate suites. Amanda's very luxurious and exquisitely decorated, and adjoining it the most modern of black-and-silver bathrooms. Judy's suite consisted of a charming bedroom and bathroom and a comfortable little sitting room overlooking the tennis courts. There were a desk and plenty of books ready for her.

Judy gasped and shook her head at her cousin.

'It's all so lovely! And enormous. Like a great hotel. I'm sure I shall never be able to manage.'

'Oh yes, you will,' said Amanda airily. 'Have a rest and change, and then you can be introduced to the staff.'

'Won't they hate me!'

'No, they'll like you,' said Amanda, who was determined that Judy should remain and remove the burden of all unattractive domestic duties from her shoulders.

'And where is your husband?'

'Away at the moment. He should be back tonight. I'll leave you to cope with him. I've got a date with a friend of mine — a man called Edward Traill. You'll probably see a lot of Eddy here. He's a great polo-player and tremendous fun. Rides divinely. He's coming up from town, and I'm dining out with him. You can tell Ricky when you see him that I'm at a party. He won't ask any questions.'

Judy looked a little gravely at her cousin. So that was how the land lay! Amanda had her men friends, went where she liked, did what she liked, and when her husband came home after having been away, she just wouldn't bother to be here to meet him. That seemed somehow an unattractive scheme of things. Not marriage as Judy would have liked it. What use all the magnificence and money without love? Perhaps she was an idealistic little fool, but she would rather have had a cottage and a man she loved, thought Judy.

Then the thought of Dickon seared her heart like a red-hot pain. Oh, Dickon, where was he? Did he feel as depressed and flat as she did? And was his marriage like this one of Amanda's — sterile and unhappy? Did he go home to find no wife awaiting him? Certainly, he had told her that he led a gay and useless life, and that it was all a hollow mockery. Judy could well believe it, if his existence bore any resemblance to the one which Amanda and her husband appeared to lead.

Amanda Portal, bone-lazy herself, had her moments of being kind, and noticed suddenly that her cousin looked very white and fatigued. She told her to lie down and have a rest before bothering to see the staff.

'All the ordering's done for today. Take it easy, old thing. Start your work tomorrow. And if you feel like it, come down to the drawing room and have a cocktail with me at six-thirty before I go.'

Judy stood at the open door of her

bedroom and watched Amanda's tall, willowy form glide down the passage. The embodiment of grace, of soignée beauty, in an ice-blue backless dress which fitted her like a glove. Smooth brown back, brown smooth legs, and scarlet sandals showing the red, lacquered nails.

Judy could well imagine men falling in love with Amanda — loving her to distraction, but getting no comfort out of that love. She would just dance her way gracefully into their lives as she danced through life, charming, careless, oblivious of whom she hurt in the process.

'If last night had happened to Amanda,' thought Judy, 'she would have taken it as an amusing pastime — not seriously, as I've done.'

Suddenly she felt no pleasure in the beauty of this luxurious house and the prospect of having quite a good time here. She felt lost and lonely. And she wanted Dickon — wanted to find herself back in that little country inn

— sitting in front of the peat fire, with Dickon's arms about her, and Dickon's magic voice weaving spells for her, catching her in the meshes of an enchantment from which she could never now escape.

She threw herself down on her bed and dissolved into tears.

4

The afternoon was hot and still. Judy, worn out, slept at last. She felt more refreshed by late afternoon. And she found plenty to do. Having introduced herself to the staff and interviewed them all, she soon discovered that there would be much that she could put right. The head-parlourmaid was a nice capable girl, willing to help, but some of the under-servants wanted controlling. One was leaving — and there was a new kitchen-maid to be found, and a neglected linen cupboard to look over. Judy settled down to straightening things out, and even replied to some of the correspondence with tradesmen, or charity requests which Amanda had flung on her desk. She thus satisfied herself that she was at 'White Monks' to some purpose, and was going to earn her bread-and-butter.

At half-past six, having changed into her one and only decent dinner-dress, she went downstairs to the drawing room and walked through one of the tall windows on to the terrace.

The sun was still shining and it was warm and beautiful. The air was full of birdsong and the fragrance of roses. So much loveliness filled Judy with a queer melancholy and made her heart ache in her breast. But she tried not to think about Dickon. Amanda's husband would be home soon. Rather rotten of Amanda to go out tonight of all nights. And most embarrassing for her, Judy, to have to introduce herself to Richard Portal and entertain him for the evening. Not that she intended to do much entertaining, because the moment the meal was over she would slip away. She was sure he wouldn't want to be bothered with her. Anyway, he mightn't come alone. Amanda said he often brought a couple of men with him. They had a squash court at 'White Monks', and a big swimming-pool.

Amanda said Ricky was fond of fresh air and exercise.

Or he might even bring a 'girlfriend', she had also said, with a hard little laugh to prove that she didn't care.

Judy hoped fervently that there wouldn't be a 'girlfriend' tonight. It would make it so awkward for her.

She heard Amanda's voice behind her.

'Oh, there you are, Judy. Come in and have a drink. I've just got five minutes before I go. I told Eddy six-forty-five.'

Judy turned and followed her cousin through the French windows into the drawing room, where the butler had placed a tray with a shaker and two glasses.

Amanda was looking as if she had stepped straight from the film *Things To Come*. Black slinky satin dress and Cellophane tunic with huge stiff sleeves! Black sandal shoes and sheer silk stockings. Over her arm she carried a silver fox cape. Lovely and extravagant, Judy thought.

'I was just looking at the garden,' Judy told her. 'It's all so beautiful, I feel I've come to paradise.'

'Oh, it's all right for a time, and particularly in the summer,' said Amanda. 'But as a permanent parking-ground it's too deadly for words.' She shook a cocktail and handed one to Judy, adding: 'Tell me what you think of this. It's my own special concoction. We call it 'White Monks Ruin'.'

Judy laughed, took the cocktail and sipped it.

It had a kick to it that made her gasp.

'Like it?' Amanda asked, and drank one, then two, and three without blenching.

'H'm,' said Judy. 'It's rather strong, isn't it?'

'I like them strong,' Amanda laughed. 'But if you're not used to them, perhaps you'd rather not finish yours.'

'Well, I don't often get the opportunity to go to cocktail parties,' said Judy.

'I can see you've led a sheltered life, my child. Cocktails are an acquired taste, anyway. I can't get Ricky to appreciate them. He prefers sherry.'

There came the sound of a car in the drive. Amanda lit a cigarette and sauntered to the window.

'That may be Eddy,' she said, looking out into the drive. But as the car rounded the bend and came into view, she came back into the room again, saying in a slightly bored tone: 'No — it's only Ricky. He's home early.'

Judy felt rather curious to see Ricky Portal. She was thankful that he had come back before Amanda went out. She could then at least introduce them, before leaving them alone for the evening. Judy put down her drink and walked to the window, and looked out as Amanda had done.

She stayed perfectly still for an instant. Her cheeks were scarlet. This was the biggest shock of her life. She had to grip the framework of the French windows to support herself, while her heart beat so wildly that she wondered if she would faint.

A large sports car had drawn up outside the front entrance. *A black-and-silver Bentley*. And the man climbing out of it was *Dickon*. Dickon, who had never been out of her thoughts since last night. Surely Dickon wasn't, *couldn't be*, Amanda's husband! A vivid blush spread over her face and neck. She was thankful that Amanda couldn't see it, as she had her back to her. She said in a hesitating voice:

'Is that — *Ricky* — your husband?'

'Yes, it is,' said Amanda. 'Sorry to leave you for the evening, darling. Don't let him bore you *too* much.'

Judy closed her eyes for an instant. Bore her! As if she could ever be bored with Dickon! If Amanda only knew! What a frightful thing to have happened. Dickon and Ricky were one and the same person. What a fool she had been not to have guessed! Of course the names were both likely contractions of 'Richard'. And he was *Amanda's husband*. The husband with whom she did not get on, and whom she left frequently in order to spend her evenings with another man! No wonder Dickon had told her that his life was empty and futile. Judy could understand everything he had said to her now.

With an immense effort she pulled herself together, turned back to Amanda and tried to behave normally. She wanted to warn Dickon, but could not. She must just wait until he came into the room. And when he saw her here, he must receive as big a shock as she had done.

She thankfully accepted the casual invitation from Amanda: 'Help yourself to a cigarette, darling'; took one from a mirror-box on the table beside the window, and lit it. She could not control the trembling of her fingers. But the cigarette gave her confidence and steadied her nerves. She smoked furiously as she waited, through agonised seconds that seemed like hours, for Dickon to appear.

At last the door opened. He came in

with that quick, light step which she remembered. For an instant he did not see Judy.

'Hullo, Mandy,' he greeted his wife. 'You're looking very like Dietrich. Going to a party?'

'Yes, up in Town. Off any minute, darling. But before I go, I just want to introduce you to my cousin. She's come to help me keep house. Perhaps I forgot to tell you I'd asked her. Anyway, this is Judy Grant. Judy, this is my husband, Ricky.'

Richard Portal gave one glance at the girl who stood silent by the window. He started violently, then stood still. *Judy!* What on earth was she doing here? Amanda said this was her cousin, and that she had come here to keep house! Was *this* the job that Judy had told him about last night! Why in heaven's name hadn't Amanda told him before? What an *appalling* thing to have happened! Of all women in the world, why must he have fallen in love with his wife's cousin, a girl who had come to live in his own house, and whom he must see every day.

He remained staring at her as though he could not believe his eyes.

At length Judy came to his rescue. She walked across and held out her hand.

'How do you do,' she said steadily.

He recovered himself, took her hand, and returned her formal greeting. But for the merest instant their startled gaze focused upon each other, in a passionate unspoken query.

To their mutual relief there came the sound of another car in the drive, then a series of shrill impatient honks from an electric horn. Amanda picked up her bag and walked to the door.

'That'll be Eddy serenading me. So long, you two. I'm sure you'll find lots to talk about. So sorry to have to leave you, Judy dear. See you in the morning.'

Then she was gone, and Judy and Dickon were alone.

Neither spoke until the sound of the

car had died away. Then he said:

'Judy — my *dear*! What in heaven's name are you doing here?'

She gave a nervous laugh.

'Well, Dickon, now you see — this is my job — the one I told you about! An awful mess, isn't it. If I'd only known, of course I'd never have come.'

'I hadn't any idea Amanda had asked anyone to come here,' said Dickon. 'She knows I don't like paid housekeepers, so I suppose her idea was to get someone in the family, and spring it on me afterwards.'

'Well, what are we going to do?' she asked.

'God knows!' he said. 'I never connected it up with you when you told me about the job you were taking.'

'And I never dreamed that Amanda's Richard was *you*.'

'Naturally not. I only told you my mother's name for me. I'm 'Ricky' to Amanda — to my friends.'

Judy nodded dumbly. For a moment they held each other's gaze. He had an almost uncontrollable desire to snatch her in his arms and tell her that ever since he left her in the hotel, he had been torn with longing for her. Like a demon, he had driven from the hotel and the temptation of her young sweetness. This morning he had reached London, gone to his Club and slept, exhausted. He had not felt that he wanted to face Amanda and any of her admirers. He had come back to Oxford, knowing that he had been crazy, hoping to wipe out the memory of those perfect, revealing hours which he had spent with Judy. Then to find her here! Could he have dreamed of such a coincidence, or foreseen such a startling conclusion to the episode? But 'conclusion' was the wrong word, he told himself wryly. It seemed only the beginning of it.

'This is the most amazing thing that's ever happened,' he said. 'And I must blame myself for not having told you my real name last night. Not that it would have made much difference.'

'Oh, yes, it would,' said Judy. 'I wouldn't have come here if I'd known.'

'But it was your job — you'd have to take it. And thank God, I didn't stop you. I'd rather go away myself than drive you out. I know how hard you've worked. You told me how much you were looking forward to making a home with your cousin!'

'Don't be absurd,' said Judy. 'If anybody goes, it'll be me. This is *your* home.'

He ignored that. A very tender expression came into his handsome eyes. He put out a hand and touched her hair.

'My dear,' he said, 'it's almost unbelievable. You — my wife's cousin! And I've never seen or heard of you. Why haven't I? Why?'

His touch brought her both ecstasy and fear. She drew away.

'I am from the 'poor' side of the family,' she said with a shaky laugh. 'Amanda's mother and mine were sisters, but our lives were always on different planes. Amanda's family always had more money than we had, and after she married you, we didn't hear much more of her.'

'Until she remembered that you knew how to do a job of work decently, then she asked you to come here and give her more time for fun,' said Richard Portal in a hard voice which Judy had not heard from him before.

Judy felt that she must defend her cousin.

'I suppose it's a bit difficult for Amanda to get through all her social duties and run a house as well.'

Dickon recovered himself sufficiently to pay some attention to his cigarette. The colour was coming back into his face. It had ebbed away at the sight of Judy. He said:

'Let's go on to the terrace and have some sherry.'

'I think dinner's nearly ready,' said Judy doubtfully.

That made him laugh.

'If you try to run this house in an

orderly and punctual manner, my poor child, you'll be up against it. Amanda and I have no sense of time. Dinner can wait. I've got to talk to you. Go on to the terrace and I'll tell Ellis to bring drinks.'

'I've just had a sample of Amanda's brand of cocktails.'

'She didn't give you one of those frightful 'White Monk' things, did she? I can't think what she puts in them — absinthe, I should think. A couple of those would put the most hardened drinker under the table.'

Judy gave a little laugh.

'Lucky I didn't have much of it, then.'

'Well, we'll have some sherry. It's a more healthy drink,' he said, and rang the bell.

Judy went on to the terrace, seated herself under the striped umbrella, and looked blindly upon the sunlit gardens.

A suffocating sense of disaster was upon her, mingled with the purest rapture at being within sight and sound of Dickon again. She was desperately in love. And it just had to be crushed down with an iron hand. Because he was married, and to her own cousin, which fact drove him even farther away from her than he had seemed to be before.

A moment later he joined her. He made her smoke a cigarette and sip a glass of sherry. They found themselves talking, talking, as they had talked to each other last night, intimately. Only now they were no longer strangers and there was no more mystery wrapped around 'Dickon.' Everything seemed clear. Without being too blunt or too disloyal, he was explaining about his marriage to Amanda and the events of the years which had annihilated happiness for both of them.

He had been madly in love with her when they were engaged. That lithe figure, that fair, astonishing beauty, had enchanted him, and he had wanted their union to be ideal. Wanted a home like 'White Monks' with Amanda

— and children. Wanted to do something of use in the world, even though he had never had to work, because at an early age he had inherited his father's fortune.

But things hadn't happened that way. Amanda, after the honeymoon, showed plainly that she had not the slightest streak of domesticity, neither had she the maternal urge, nor real love of homelife. Spending money wantonly, and pursuing one new pleasure after another, was her idea of bliss. She was insatiable for admiration, and she got plenty. Because she was lovely and fascinating, she wooed her husband away from his own ideals. Richard Portal found his nature hardening to meet her hardness, and wasted time and money, at first with her, and later apart from her, because they seemed to have nothing in common.

'I was weak, Judy,' Richard Portal told her at the end of his story. 'I know I should have forced Amanda to take life more seriously. But I gave in to her.

And later, when I couldn't love her any more, knowing that she hadn't any love for me, I didn't bother. I just let things slide. But it's been empty, my dear. Hellish lonely in the crowd, and I've been ashamed — ashamed of my futility as well as of hers. I don't blame her any more than I blame myself. But somehow, when I met you last night, I knew what life might have been. But never with Amanda. It made me realise all the more how much I've missed. It could only have been full and beautiful and worth living — with you!'

Judy clasped her hands together. She had listened earnestly and in silence. She knew that he spoke the truth. Amanda had always been a complete egotist — pleasure mad. Judy was filled with pity. But she did not see what to do.

'It's such a muddle, Dickon. Or oughtn't I to call you that now. No, I mustn't. You must be Richard.'

'Ricky with the others,' he said impatiently. 'But I'd rather have remained

'Dickon' to you, Judy.'

'I shall think of you as that, always.'

'You got my note?'

'Yes. I meant never to part with it.'

'I was a coward to run away, but I had to.'

'I understand.'

'You understand everything. There's a lot of wisdom in that small head of yours, Judy. I wonder you don't despise me for being a coward. But I just couldn't tell you, face to face, that I was married. I was so much in love. I am still. That's the devil of it. And you? Do you feel the same as you did last night?'

Judy stood up, flinging away her cigarette-end on to the lawn below.

'Yes. But it won't do, Dickon — Ricky,' she corrected herself. 'Under the circumstances, I shall just have to go away.'

'Don't, please,' he said.

'I must. We couldn't either of us go on seeing each other. Besides — Amanda doesn't know about last night, and it wouldn't be fair to her.'

Richard Portal's tired face suddenly relaxed.

'Judy,' he said, 'I adore you for your idealism. But believe me, my dear, if Amanda did know, she wouldn't care a damn. She has her own admirers, by the plenty.'

'But it isn't right. It isn't marriage as it should be.'

'You're telling me?' he asked, using the Americanism with bitterness.

'I must go away.'

'Where? To what?'

Her heart sank a bit.

'I don't really know. I'll find another job. It'll be easier for both of us when I've gone.'

He stood beside her, resting his hands on the stone balustrade, his eyes narrowing as he looked over the serene beauty of the grounds. The sun was setting. Little gold-edged clouds moved slowly across the tranquil blue of the summer sky. The air was heavy with the luscious scent of hundreds of roses. With a deep note of pain in his voice,

81

Richard Portal said:

'I'd give anything in the world to keep you here at 'White Monks', Judy. You don't know what it meant when I walked into the house and found you here.'

'I'd like to stay. It's all so gorgeous. But you see how impossible it is.'

He turned to her. His eyes were dark and bitter.

'Oh, God, and I'm responsible for driving you away. You might have been happy here.'

'Yes.'

It was all she could say, and in a way she meant it, although she wanted to tell him that she couldn't be happy anywhere without him.

'Well, at least will you stay until you find another job?' he said. 'I wouldn't mind so much if I thought you had somewhere else to go. Swear you'll stay till you've found something else.'

'Very well,' she said miserably, and added: 'Ought we to tell — Amanda?'

'What's the use?' He shrugged his

shoulders. 'She'd only laugh and treat it as a joke, and I don't think we want a jest made of it, do we?'

She flushed hotly.

'Certainly not.'

'It was too lovely for that, Judy,' he said with a warm, revealing glance. 'Much too lovely, my dear.'

'Are you sure,' she said with difficulty, 'that if Amanda *did* find out about last night — she wouldn't think . . . '

'Wouldn't put the worst construction on it, do you mean?' he finished for her.

She nodded.

'I doubt it. Anyway, we could prove otherwise. But I'm in a mood when I wouldn't care, for myself. I'd like to take you by the hand and tell Amanda that I love you — that I wanted my freedom — for you.'

Judy gasped.

'No, no! That couldn't be right.'

'Then you don't believe in divorce, Judy?'

She had a moment of panic, not

knowing what to reply. Her principles might be against divorce, but all her emotions were for him — all her desires moved towards him.

Then suddenly she felt his hand grasp her wrist warmly and strongly. She heard him say:

'Tell me — if the question of divorce arose between Amanda and myself — would you come away with me? *Would you?* Answer me, Judy.'

5

Judy was caught up in the glamour of this man's suggestion only for a second, and then she seemed to hear her cousin Amanda's high, sweet voice saying:

'Just the same as ever, Judy. Full of ideas and high principles . . . long may you keep them . . . '

Glamour fell away from her. In a moment of sheer common sense, of judgment, she saw Dickon not as the 'mystery love' who could take her hand and lead her to enchanted heights, but as a tired, harassed young man with too much money, too much time to waste, loathing his loveless marriage, and still — Amanda's husband.

'There can be no question of divorce between you and Amanda through me — Ricky.' Judy said that unfamiliar name with difficulty. 'I could never come away with you while you're

Amanda's husband.'

The light went out of Richard Portal's eyes. He said:

'I knew you'd say that. You're so strongminded, little Judy. It's quite frightening.'

'You do understand?'

'That you think I ought to make the best of it with Amanda — yes.'

'Well, oughtn't you . . . ?' asked Judy painfully.

He cocked an eyebrow, and it gave his face a sardonic look that took away a lot of youth. And he laughed, a hard little laugh which Judy did not find good to hear. He lit another cigarette.

'I dare say. But even if I got a little encouragement — I could never love Amanda again, now that I've met you. But she doesn't help much — she likes plenty of amusement and variety, and doesn't want to settle down.'

'Poor Dickon,' said Judy softly. She thought she knew the sort of marriage Dickon would have liked. A home, and children, and a wife who was there when he came home; who would prefer to stay with him rather than dance the hours away with other men. Only too well Judy knew that he had not found, and never could find, that sort of wife in Amanda.

'I suppose it's as bad for her,' Dickon went on. 'She must find it very irritating to be tied to a husband who doesn't get on with her friends or care for her amusements. And there's a man, too, whom I think she's a bit in love with — that fellow Traill. She's probably out with him tonight. But she can't do anything about that. It isn't that her principles are so high, but she's always had plenty of money and luxury, and this man isn't well enough off to give her what she's accustomed to. No, I doubt if she will leave me for him.'

'It doesn't sound much like love to me,' said Judy.

'Amanda isn't the sort of person to fall in love with anybody to the extent of facing poverty for their sake. Not that Traill is badly off, but it's just a question of comparison. She wouldn't have nearly so much as she has as my wife, that's all.'

'It all sounds so calculating and mercenary. And anyway, that doesn't help us. The thing is, I must tell Amanda I don't like it here and get another job. The sooner I go away, the better.'

He looked at her downcast face, then at a distracting glimpse of ivory-white below the line of sunburn on her slender throat. He flushed to the roots of his hair, and a sudden anger rushed through him — anger against her, himself — Amanda — fate!

'Yes, you're right,' he said violently. 'It'll seem bad enough when you're miles out of reach, but to see you here with *her* — make comparisons — remember last night — no, that'll be too much! But get it out of your head, Judy, that I can settle down to do the right thing and sit at the feet of my wife. She wouldn't let me, if I tried. I'm not without my principles, God knows, and I've had my ideals. But perhaps I haven't found it as easy as you have to live up to them.'

Anger burnt up in her to meet his own. She looked at him with bright, resentful eyes.

'How do you know I've found it easy? I haven't! Life may have been more difficult for you in one way than it has for me, but it's all relative, isn't it? And do you suppose I found it easy to say 'no' to you just now? I didn't. I've never met anybody like you in my life before — never had any of this . . . ' She made a sweeping gesture with her hand indicating the house and the grounds. 'But you're Amanda's husband. And she's my cousin, and she's given me a job. So long as I'm here, I've got to remember it. Oh, I think I *hate* you for making me love you at all.'

Her outburst was somehow as much of a relief to him as it was to her. He understood it. Her anger he could bear, but not that last unhappy cry. Swiftly he caught her hand.

'Don't say that, darling, please. Don't hate me for last night or for anything. I'm all sorts of a cad, I suppose, and you're right — everything you've said is right. I'm sorry. Forget it, and for God's sake let's be friends, even if we can't be lovers.'

She pressed his hands with hers and nodded dumbly. Her eyes were full of hot tears. And suddenly she snatched her fingers away and turned, groping for a handkerchief.

'Dinner will spoil,' she said in a choked voice. 'Hadn't you better have it? Please forgive me if I don't come down. I'm awfully tired. I think I ought to go straight to bed.'

He did not try to stop her. He was as miserable as she was. He knew that it would only be a strain for them to spend that long summer's evening together.

Judy went up to her sitting room, cried her eyes out, and paid little attention to the food that one of the maids brought up to her. She cried because she loved that man downstairs quite desperately and she knew it. Cried because she knew that she could never hate him, but must love him whatever he had done. And who was she, she asked herself, to judge? The life he had led with Amanda was so different from any that she, herself, had known. They were rich and spoiled. They had never worked or saved and made sacrifices for each other. They had grown slack and egotistical, and fallen out of love — if, indeed, they had ever honestly been in love!

Of course Amanda seemed, so far as Judy could see, to have her compensations. Amanda led a gay, exciting life. That was because she skimmed over the surface of things and never delved underneath. But there was more in Dickon. (Judy could only think of him as Dickon.) He was sick of things as they were, lonely, and asking more of life. She, Judy, could, have given him the home, the children he craved. Gladly she would have followed him to the ends of the earth. Without any of his money — but just with blind devotion like a gipsy woman follows her lover. But she had to deny him everything and deny herself. It seemed such a tragedy.

It took Judy a good many hours to settle down to the realisation that she must leave 'White Monks', and find another job — just as soon as she could. She would really much rather have run away tonight and been saved the torture of seeing Dickon day by day, knowing that she must starve him and herself. But she had promised him that she would stay until she found something else.

She was much too tired and over-wrought to write letters tonight. Tomorrow she would apply to one or two agencies in London who knew her and ask if there were any domestic or secretarial jobs going.

Several times that evening Judy felt tempted to go downstairs and speak to Dickon, but she restrained the impulse.

Later, when it was dusk, from her sitting room window she saw him going towards the swimming-pool, wearing a blue bathgown, a towel slung round his neck. And although she could not see the pool, she heard a sudden splash, and could imagine him diving into the water. Something exulted in her at the thought of the youth and grace and good looks of him; all his charm. Even though she would never belong to him, it was fine to know that he loved her and would have had her by his side always, if he could.

When finally she was in bed, restless and unhappy, she heard a soft tap on her door. She sat up, her heart pounding. She heard Dickon's voice:

'Are you awake, Judy?'

'Yes.'

'I just want to tell you something.'

'Yes?'

'I think your courage magnificent, and I wish I had a tenth of it. You've taught me something, Judy. I won't forget it — or you. Good night.'

She swallowed hard.

'Good night.'

Came his low voice:

'I'll do what I can about Amanda — because you've asked me to. Good night.'

And then he was gone. Judy's heart-beats quietened down and she flung herself back on the pillow, pressing her face against it, and struggled with a sudden demon of jealousy. Wild jealousy of Amanda. Amanda who was his wife. He was going to 'do what he could about her,' he said. That meant he would try to be happy with her. And she, Judy, had wished it that way. It was the right thing. But all that was humanly weak in her rebelled fiercely against the very thought of Amanda in Dickon's arms. It was right, oh yes, and grand of Dickon, but she couldn't bear to dwell on the thought of it.

She wondered feverishly what excuse she could make to Amanda for going just as soon as she had arrived at 'White Monks'.

She decided that it would be best to get the other job all settled before she told Amanda of her intention. It would appear so ungrateful, after Amanda's kindness in bringing her here. But she could never explain — never!

In the morning Judy was up almost as early as the staff. With a fresh green overall over her dress, she set to work to do all the flowers. Amanda, she was informed by Ellis, was never called until she rang, after a late night. Mr. Portal was out riding.

The talkative butler enlarged on the subject of Mr. Portal. How well he looked on a horse, how magnificently he rode, what a splendid gentleman he was, and Judy, arranging a mass of pink roses in a great crystal bowl, listened wistfully. She thought:

'So he was up early, too. Perhaps, like me — he just couldn't sleep.'

It was eleven o'clock before she saw either her cousin or Dickon.

When Judy first walked into her cousin's suite, she heard Dickon's voice in the bedroom and knew that he was there with Amanda. She hesitated a moment. Then heard Amanda's voice:

'Don't be a fool, my dear. What does it matter to you whether I was out with Eddy or not? Much too late to start criticising my behaviour or my friends.'

From Dickon:

'Isn't it time we pulled ourselves together, Mandy? I see less of you in this house than I do of the servants.'

'What about it? We don't like the same people or the same things, Ricky. We agreed to differ. For God's sake, don't start interfering. You've tons of friends.'

'Has it ever struck you that I might want something more?'

Judy's cheeks burned. She felt she should go and yet was rooted to the spot. She was agonised for Dickon. And horribly ashamed for Amanda. Selfish, heartless Amanda. When her answer came it was not very attractive. It brought an even deeper red to Judy's face.

'My dear Ricky — since you've got a fit of loneliness, it may please you that my dear little cousin Judy has come to live with us. She'll run 'White Monks' beautifully, and perhaps make a nice soothing companion for you, into the bargain.'

Judy turned to fly, but it was too late. Richard Portal emerged from his wife's bedroom. He was white under his tan and shaking, but Judy had never seen him look more handsome than in his riding kit. Such a boy with that silk spotted muffler round his throat. As he marched past her, he flung her a dark, bitter look.

'Maybe you heard,' he said under his breath. 'Amanda would like you to make a 'nice soothing companion' for me. And you want there to be peace between us. *God!*'

Judy shook her head helplessly. Then he was gone. Amanda called out:

'Is that you, Judy?'

Judy walked into the bedroom. Amanda was drinking her tea, sitting up in her luxurious bed with a pink swans-down cape over a chiffon nightdress. The peach-coloured quilted spread was littered with papers and letters. Amanda's pet Pekinese, a white ball of snowy fur, was curled up beside her. Amanda looked lovely, fatigued, and irritable. Gravely Judy regarded her, wondering why anybody as lovely should be quite so cruel.

'Thank God, you've come,' said Amanda. 'Ricky's in a foul mood. I need petting. Say something nice to me, darling.'

Judy tried to say something nice, but the words stuck in her throat. But she could not forbear asking:

'Why was he — foul?'

'Oh, interfering. I loathe being interfered with,' said Amanda, and flung herself back on her pillow.

Judy put her hands in the pockets of her overall and stared at the floor. She felt uncomfortable and miserable. There were so many things that she wanted to say to Amanda and could not.

'You might as well know,' continued Amanda, 'that my charming husband and I do not get on, and it's no use pretending we do.'

'I can't think why,' said Judy, keeping her head bent so that Amanda should not see her eyes.

Amanda gave a little laugh.

'I suppose Ricky attracts you. He attracts all women. But when you know him better, my dear, you'll find he's full of ideals, and no woman could live up to them.'

'I wouldn't have thought that,' said Judy in a low voice. 'He seems so — easy.'

'Perhaps I'm the one at fault,' said Amanda, shrugging her beautiful shoulders. 'Because I don't like domesticity, as I told you yesterday. Ricky can be a lot of fun when he wants to be, but when that 'let's settle down in front of the fireside' mood comes over him, I just can't cope.'

Judy made no reply. She could have said something extremely sharp and scornful. She began to see how hopeless the whole thing was from Dickon's point of view.

'How did you and Ricky get on last night?' asked Amanda casually.

'Quite well . . . ' The words stuck in Judy's throat.

'I'm glad you're here,' said Amanda. 'I'm sure you'll be a great help to me in lots of ways.'

Judy made no comment. But she sent up a secret prayer to heaven that she'd find another job quickly.

Amanda gave Judy a list of the things that she wished her to do today. She was lavish with praise of her work last night. And she had an unexpectedly generous side. Before Judy left the room, she insisted upon her taking an armful of lovely, quite new clothes which Amanda said she was 'tired of'. She seemed to have taken a liking to the cousin, who was so different from herself in every respect. And in a queer way Judy had to like Amanda, even though she could not respect her. But she could see what a devastating effect a woman like Amanda could have upon a man as sensitive as Dickon.

Amanda went out to lunch. Judy, to her embarrassment, yet secret delight, found herself lunching alone with Dickon. He looked pale and was detached and quiet, as though drawn into himself after the fruitless attempt he had made this morning to get on better terms with Amanda.

Whilst the servants were present he spoke to Judy impersonally and with an exquisite politeness which somehow hurt her, although she felt a fool for being hurt. As soon as the coffee had been served and they were alone, he offered her a cigarette. As he leaned forward with the little gold lighter, he looked into her eyes. Then the ice seemed to melt. Under his breath he said:

'My dear!'

The scarlet flags of emotion were hoisted high in her cheeks then. She said:

'I — I must go and do some household accounts.'

He leant back and laughed a little.

'Conscientious child!'

'Will you be in for dinner?' she asked.

'Is this in order that you may count the chops, or are you just anxious to know whether you will have my company?'

'You're being horrid,' said Judy.

'My wife will tell you that I *am* horrid.'

'But you're not!' broke out Judy hotly. 'You're so terribly nice.'

He looked suddenly weary but very tender.

'I seem to remember you saying that to me before — and it's grand to have a champion like yourself. Perhaps you're right. Perhaps I *am* nice, but nobody knows it except you. God, Judy, I wish I had the chance to show you what I *could* be — *could* do for you . . . '

He broke of, and added:

'Oh, what's the use? As much use saying things like that to you, as trying to make Amanda change her attitude towards life and me.'

Judy looked at him in silent distress. He gave her another warm look from his handsome eyes and moved away from her.

'Is Amanda going to be in this evening?'

Judy's heart beat painfully, her gaze following his tall graceful figure.

'Amanda is dining at home. I believe — Major Traill is dining here too.'

'Well, if Traill's dining here, I shall be out,' said Dickon abruptly, and walked from the room.

She knew that he was wretched. His whole attitude was so tired, so cynical. How maddening of Amanda to turn him into such a person. More than maddening — it was a crime, thought Judy.

Later, she heard Dickon drive away in the Bentley and wondered where he was going; what amusement he would find as an anodyne from the torment of his thoughts; whether he would take some woman out to dine. Poor frustrated Dickon. Judy's thoughts went with him, pursued him in an agony of frustration that must almost equal his. It was so awful to love him and not be able to help him.

She could not bring herself to be present at dinner that night. She decorated the dinner-table with pink carnations, saw that everything was perfect, then went to her own suite, leaving a suitable excuse for Amanda, which she felt certain would be appreciated.

Sheer curiosity made her watch from her window and take a look at Amanda's present 'flame' when he arrived.

Edward Traill seemed quite ordinary — the antithesis of Dickon. A big-boned, fair man with square military shoulders and fair moustache. Sleek and apparently amusing enough for Amanda, since they were laughing together as they stepped out of her car. And as they walked into the house,

Judy heard Amanda say:

'I'm dying for a drink. Tell Ellis to shake us a cocktail, Eddy, there's a lamb!'

The 'lamb' retorted:

'I see we have two minds with but a single thought, lady mine.'

They disappeared, and Judy turned back to her room, her ears tingling. How dared he speak like that to Amanda! 'Lady mine', indeed! Amanda belonged to Dickon, not to Edward Traill. Why did Amanda see no wrong in bringing this man here, knowing that it drove Dickon out?

Judy went to bed that second night at 'White Monks' almost as wretched as she had been on the first.

There followed a succession of unhappy days in which her patience with Amanda was stretched so taut that it came near to snapping, and her love and pity for Dickon drenched her until she felt herself drowning. She wondered how long it would be before her emotions wore her down and she would run to him, knowing full well that his arms would open to receive her. Every time he looked at her his eyes were like dark rapiers of fiery light, penetrating her imagination, burning her up. She knew that he loved her and wanted her. It was so difficult, in the face of all that went on at 'White Monks', not to show him how much she loved him, too.

It seemed like a malicious whim of Fate that no other job was forthcoming. The agencies where she had applied could find her nothing at the moment. There were hundreds of women wanting work, they said, and not enough jobs to meet the demand.

6

By the end of the month Judy was running 'White Monks' just as efficiently as Amanda had prophesied that she would do. There was peace amongst the staff, order in the linen room, and a tidiness in Amanda's desk that had never existed before. Judy brought her up-to-date with all her correspondence, which — Amanda laughingly announced — was unique.

And as was inevitable, Amanda reached a pitch where she felt she could not do without her capable and tactful cousin, and wondered how she had ever managed before she came. She continued to show a curiously kind side to Judy. She liked her personally. Admired her. And she wanted to include her in the parties that took place at 'White Monks'. But with one or two exceptions, when Amanda was insistent, Judy managed to avoid them. She felt out of place in the gay, flippant, fashionable throng of men and women surrounding Amanda.

As for Dickon, she saw little of him. More often than not he was in Town for the day. If he was at 'White Monks', and there were 'parties' going, he was drawn into them by Amanda. She had no use for him as a husband, but she knew that he was immensely popular with other women, and she liked him to act the graceful host.

Judy, looking on, watched Dickon, and her heart ached for him. He could drink with the rest of them, laugh, jest, dance. He played squash, rode, or swam, and lazed when the weather permitted. And when it did not, he was always ready indoors for a poker party or some Contract Bridge. But Judy knew that he hated it all — that he felt as alone in that crowd as she, Judy, would feel. And this was his marriage. What a travesty! When Dickon laughed, Judy could have wept for him.

Major Traill haunted the house. By now Judy had met him, even talked to him. She could not actively dislike him, except on Dickon's account. Traill was really a very likeable and charming man, and he seemed no worse than the rest of the crowd, none of whom had much aim and object in life, so far as Judy could see, except to enjoy themselves. And perhaps, she told herself, there was no real harm in his relationship with Amanda. It was just the way of these men and women to call each other 'darling' and flirt outrageously. Perhaps Amanda was, in her fashion, quite faithful to Dickon. Judy did not know. But she became aware with every passing day that it was vitally necessary for her to get away from 'White Monks'.

The times when she saw Dickon by himself were difficult and strained. Once, when they came face to face alone, he took her hand, looked down at her with his tired eyes and said:

'Not enjoying being here much, are

you, little Judy?'

'No,' was her vehement answer.

'And I don't think I want you to stay,' he said in a low voice. 'It drives me crazy. I think of you upstairs in your room, and I want to get away from the crowds and come up and sit at your feet and put my head in your lap and sleep!'

Her heart seemed to break for him. She could find nothing to say — only press his fingers and run away before her feelings got the better of her.

Another week passed by. There was always much to do at 'White Monks' — so much that the time seemed to fly, despite Judy's mental conflict and her restlessness. But still no sign of another job. The longer she stayed, the more awkward it grew, since Amanda continually expressed her appreciation of Judy.

'I couldn't possibly go on without you now, darling,' she said to her cousin one evening, when Judy sat in a darkened bedroom, massaging cream into Amanda's face. Amanda liked Judy to do that during her hour's rest, before she changed for dinner. It soothed her.

Tonight something impelled Judy to speak of Dickon. Gathering up her courage, she said:

'Amanda, do you think Ricky looks — very well?'

Amanda yawned and said that she hadn't noticed.

'I don't think he does,' said Judy. 'Amanda, why don't you have a quiet evening with him sometime? It would do you both good.'

Amanda lifted her heavy lashes and looked languidly at Judy.

'My dear girl — it would bore us both to tears.'

'Perhaps you're wrong. Perhaps it wouldn't bore him.'

'Judy darling, you're too divine! So full of romance that doesn't really exist.'

Judy wanted to cry out:

'You're wrong. It *does*! And you're missing it — passing it by — and stealing it from Dickon, too. When

111

you're both old, you'll realise what you've missed. It isn't fair on *him*.'

But she said nothing. She went on massaging Amanda's lovely, hard young face, knowing that her one feeble little effort on Dickon's behalf had failed. And what was the use, anyhow? Perhaps Dickon didn't want evenings alone with Amanda any more. Perhaps he couldn't love her again. And Judy could not feel guilty about that. She had taken nothing from Amanda. Amanda had driven Dickon from her long before she, Judy, came into his life.

At the beginning of July, the Portals held the big dance which they gave in their country home every year. Little expense was spared in order to make it a success. And Judy was to remember that dance all her life. Not only because she helped do much of the work before it, but because of what happened — afterwards.

She was not allowed to run away from *this* party. She must dance every dance, Amanda told her, and Dickon himself, when he saw her during the morning, said:

'You're going to dance with me tonight, Judy, so don't forget it!'

The ball was a thrilling affair. The weather had been windy and wet for several days, but had the grace to change on the night of the dance. It was fine and warm. A moon came out, and all the long windows in the drawing-room were wide open to the beautiful gardens, where cunning lights shone from the trees, making it look like fairyland. The swimming pool was floodlit for those who liked midnight bathing.

A special band came down from London and played strenuously. The drawing room, cleared of furniture, was decorated with roses, carnations, and lilies, and great palms from the hot-houses at 'White Monks'. On the terrace, which had been banked with blue and pink hydrangeas, there were lighted tables for supper.

Of the hundreds of guests that came

Judy knew only a few who were regular visitors to 'White Monks'. Edward Traill amongst them, of course. And the gallant Major was never far from the side of his hostess, who looked her loveliest, Judy had to admit. Angry she might be with Amanda, jealous of the chances that Amanda had had with Dickon, and thrown away, but nobody could deny her loveliness and her charm, when she chose to exert it. She was all in white. She looked incapable of wrongdoing, Judy thought a little sentimentally, in her dazzling white dress and with a coronet of gardenias about her golden head. There was something pure and ethereal about her. And she danced divinely. But Richard Portal had no eyes for his wife. He was not to be moved by her physical appeal. He knew that if he asked her for a dance, he would receive a flippant refusal, which would jar rather than disappoint. So he went where his heart directed — to Judy.

There was nothing dazzling about

Judy. But when he found her in the crowd and took her in his arms for their first dance, no other woman in the room seemed to exist for him any longer. Dear little Judy! Quite a beautiful Judy tonight in that mist-grey chiffon dress which had been one of Amanda's expensive creations, and which Judy had altered cleverly for herself. It drooped a little off the shoulders, and had a Victorian posy of scarlet flowers at the breast. It suited Judy's dark hair and her warm colouring. And Amanda had made her pin a red flower in her brown curls. Dickon looked down into shy hazel eyes and pressed her close to him.

'My darling!' he said against her hair. 'You look adorable.'

It was the first time she had heard him call her 'Darling' since the night when she had fallen in love with him — when she had thought of him as her lover, *hers*. For a moment she responded to the sheer rapture of their dance. For her there was nobody in that room, or on earth, except this young god with his grey, ardent eyes, his smooth black head, his white tie and tails; this man whom all other women in the world must envy her.

Two, three, four dances they had together. And Judy had never known that dancing could be so sweet. A man in the band sang through the microphone which had been arranged for him:

'*The touch of your lips upon my brow* —
Your lips that are cool and sweet;
Such tenderness lightens their soft caress.
My heart forgets to beat . . . '

Judy hardly dared look at Dickon, till at last he forced her to do so, and when their gaze met, she felt, indeed, her heart almost stand still. Her face was suddenly drained of colour.

'I can't dance any more — I can't,' she whispered. 'Let me go, Dickon.'

'No,' he said. 'Why should I? I'm sick of this pretence — this farce about Amanda. You and I were meant for each other. Judy, I . . . '

'Please, Dickon, don't!' she broke in. 'You promised — and you know we can do nothing about it.'

With a violent effort he regained his emotional balance. She saw the mask drop back over his face. Something seemed to die in him. She saw that, too, and wondered how she would be strong enough to go through with it. He said:

'You're quite right. I seem to do nothing but tell you I'm sorry for what I've done. Let's go and have a cigarette and a drink, and talk about the Wimbledon finals.'

In miserable silence she walked with him through the hall, away from the music and the dancing towards the supper room. They had to pass through a small, tapestried anteroom which was dimly lit by candles, and had been fitted up with sofas and chairs for sitting-out.

When Judy and Dickon entered this

room, they came unexpectedly upon a man and a woman who were on the sofa locked in a close embrace. Judy drew back hurriedly.

'We aren't wanted here,' she whispered.

Dickon did not answer. She saw the expression on his face, glanced again quickly at the lovers who were still oblivious of their entry, and then her heart gave a hot throb of shame and embarrassment. The woman, in white, lovely, golden-haired, was Amanda. The man kissing her was Edward Traill.

Back in the hall, Judy did not know which way to look or what to say, but Dickon said it for her.

'*Most* awkward! But of course one realises what goes on without needing an exhibition of it.'

'Oh, I wish I could do something, Dickon,' said Judy frantically.

'You can do nothing. And you have asked me to go on dedicating my life to *that*, so I'll do so.'

'Not to that! Oh, why don't you

make Amanda see sense!'

'I've tried till I'm sick of trying. If I kicked the man out of the house, she'd find somebody else. I think in her way she's fond of him, but he hasn't got much money . . . ' Dickon laughed under his breath. 'But one day — if I don't leave her first — she may leave me, for a millionaire.'

Judy said:

'I shall go — I shall go away tomorrow. I can't stand any more of this.'

'All right, go if you must. I have no right to stop you,' he said.

They stood looking at each other, both violently disturbed and miserable. And suddenly he caught her close and kissed her on the lips, as he had kissed her that night in the inn.

'Always I'll love you — *always*!' he said, and left her standing there in a kind of daze.

She covered her face with her hands. She could not go to that ballroom and dance with any other man. She felt furiously ashamed for Dickon — ashamed of Amanda.

In the candlelit room through the archway, Amanda Portal drew back from Edward Traill's embrace and demanded a cigarette.

'This won't do!' she said with a flippant laugh which generally covered some deeper feeling in Amanda.

Major Traill passed a white silk handkerchief over his face, then handed her a cigarette-case.

'You're right, lady mine. It won't.'

'I think,' said Amanda, herself applying the match to the cigarette with slender fingers that were not quite steady, 'I think, Eddy, that we've reached a crisis.'

'We've been facing one for months, my dear girl. We've lived on the edge of a precipice, lord knows.'

'Well, we've tumbled over it tonight,' said Amanda.

The man looked at her with some perplexity. He was madly in love with Amanda Portal. He supposed that he had no right to be — she was another man's wife. Yet on her own admission, and on the face of things, she and Richard Portal did not get on. They did not understand each other. Portal was a 'damn good chap' in the Major's estimation. But he took himself too seriously. And he wanted to take Mandy seriously too, which was fatal. Nobody should take Mandy seriously. She was just a gay, lazy, lovely thing who wanted continual amusing. Nothing fireside or domestic, and none of this 'let's build a home' tune which Portal had wanted to sing. Of course she'd got Portal where she wanted him now. He made no demands on her. But they were neither of them content. And Traill was positive that he could make Amanda completely happy.

He was older than Portal. Much older than Amanda. He delighted in petting her; spoiling her. There was no darn silly thing that she wanted to do that he wouldn't agree to. He was helplessly and hopelessly in love.

Polo and pretty women had always been Edward Traill's two great passions in life, and today, lovely, spoiled Amanda, so exquisitely fair, so devastatingly attractive, came first. Unfortunately he hadn't as much money as Ricky Portal. His private income was a fairly stout one, but not stout enough to stand up to polo ponies — and Amanda! Something would have to go. He didn't want it to be Amanda. On the other hand, he was afraid that it she thought he had to economise in any direction, it would chill her regard for him. He knew his Mandy. She loved luxury just as a cat loves cream.

'And why have we gone over the edge tonight, my angel?' he asked her. 'Portal isn't fed up with me for hanging round, is he?'

'Very fed up, I dare say, but that's not the question. *I'm* the one who's fed up.'

Traill fingered his moustache nervously.

'With me?'

She turned to him and put both

hands out with a sudden, lost, 'little girl' look in her limpid eyes which she could muster at times, and which never failed to bring Traill on to his knees before her.

'Never with you, Eddy. You're grand. You're the only one who understands me. But I'm fed up with the position. It wouldn't be so bad if I thought Ricky cared for some girl the way I care for you. I'd feel happier about things. But he's lonely and miserable. I know it. You may think I'm hard and callous about him. But I'm not.'

'It isn't your fault that you can't be in love with him.'

'But it is my fault if I hang on to our marriage just because I like what I get out of it. I'm beginning to despise myself.'

Traill was astonished, and looked it. Amanda was showing a new, soft side tonight. He thought it rather touching of her to worry about Portal. He raised both her hands to his lips.

'My lovely lady! Why not come away

with me? I've asked you so many times. I know I can't give you what Portal does. But we could have quite a good time together.'

Amanda drew her hands away and stood up.

'Oh, I don't know!' she said. '*I don't know!* We'll talk about it some other time; later perhaps. Now I must get back to my guests.'

When Amanda returned to the ballroom, she found that her cousin had gone to bed, and Ricky, with a rather wooden expression, was being the dutiful host, dancing every dance.

7

Meanwhile Judy, up in her room in the darkness stood gazing out of the window. But she was blind to the beauty of the moonlit garden. Neither did she hear the murmur of voices that penetrated from below, mingled with the rhythm of a dance tune. The festivities were still in full swing, but she had rushed upstairs after Dickon had left her, feeling she could not bear to stay down there another minute.

Her thoughts were mixed and chaotic as she reviewed the events of the evening. She thrilled again for a moment, to the memory of the dances she and Dickon had had together, when he had held her close to him for the first time since the night at the inn.

Then came the recollection of the discovery of Amanda in Edward Traill's arms. Amanda, oblivious of them, or of anything but her lover. Judy wondered how she could be so shameless. How could she behave so outrageously with another man in her husband's house, and especially at a time like tonight, when any of their guests might have walked in and seen them?

Judy realised suddenly that it would be futile and impossible for Dickon to attempt to make a fresh start with Amanda. She was far too egotistical to bother about him, or even to ask herself for one moment whether she was playing the game or making him happy. Such a thought would never enter her head. She did what she liked. Ricky could do the same — so long as he left her to go her own way and have her own friends — and lovers, if she wanted them. Judy knew, too, that Amanda would even welcome the suggestion that her husband was interested in another woman, because it would balance her own 'affair', and deprive him of the right to criticise her.

And that was what made things so

hard. There was every opportunity for Judy and Dickon to be thrown together, and only too few obstacles — except the one that was insuperable to them because of their principles. Dickon's marriage. A mere molehill to Amanda, who had no principles.

Judy decided that she must get away — at once. She wouldn't wait for the morning. She dared not see Dickon again. Neither could she face a scene with Amanda — numerous questions, explanations, lies — for she would have to lie, since she could not tell her the truth, or give her the real reason why she was leaving 'White Monks'. She would pack now, and leave in 'Muggins' as soon as the dance was over. She would write a note for Amanda, giving any excuse she could think of.

Judy felt her way to the electric-light switch by the door and pressed it. The sudden illumination after the darkness made her blink for a minute. Her eyes were stinging with tears.

As she packed, she heard cars being driven down the drive. So the party was over at last! When everything was quiet again, it would be safe for her to leave. She took off her evening dress and shoes and packed them, and closed the case. Then she put on a suit and walking shoes. As she sat down to write the note to Amanda, she decided that it was best to give no actual excuse, because she could think of none that would sound convincing. And anyway, by the time Amanda received the note, she, Judy, would be in London, beyond the reach of reproaches and questions. Amanda must think what she liked of her behaviour. She wrote:

'Dear Amanda,
I'm afraid this will be a surprise to you, and I'm terribly sorry for letting you down, but I'm leaving early this morning. I can't explain — please believe that I must go for a vital reason, and forgive me.

Judy.'

She put it into an envelope and addressed it to 'Mrs. Portal.'

It was three o'clock by the time Judy switched off her light and, opening the door, looked into the passage. It was quite dark. Judy had a torch with her and flashed the beam guardedly towards the wide staircase. In the hall she stopped to leave the note for Amanda on the large oak table. One of the servants would see it there in the morning and send it up on Amanda's breakfast tray.

In the feeble light of the torch, the hall presented a queer, depressing look. There were drooping flowers and empty glasses everywhere, and that queer mixture of stale odours peculiar to the aftermath of a party.

Judy was thankful when she closed the heavy front door behind her and breathed the soft fresh air again. She had no need to use the torch out here, for the garden was flooded with the light of a full moon. She made her way round to the garage, started up

'Muggins', and was soon driving out of the gates of 'White Monks' on to the main road.

She drove slowly in the direction of London. The hood of the car was down. She took deep breaths of the sweet-scented air. The road stretched before her — a pale silver strip with black grotesque shadows of trees and bushes lying across it in sharp contrast. A lovely, peaceful world — like a beautiful symphony.

If only life around had been in tune with it, Judy thought! But in her particular world, it was a symphony of discords tonight. In fact, the whole situation was rather like a badly played piece of music. Full of mistakes that, once made, were made for ever, no matter how much one tried to correct them. Amanda's marriage to Dickon. That had been the first mistake. The first wrong note. Dickon's unselfish, peace-loving temperament jarred with Amanda's pleasure mad, egotistical one.

And then Judy had met Dickon. But if only she had met him at the right time, their lives would have harmonised well enough. But it had all happened much too late. Like striking one note of a chord after the others have been struck, spoiling the rhythm.

Judy laughed a little sadly to herself. She could go on enlarging on that theme for ever. If she was going to liken Amanda, herself, and Dickon to notes in a piece of music, she could wonder what became of the notes after they had been played. Did they die utterly and become a mere memory? Was that what must happen to her love for Dickon? Who was to know?

But in the meantime she had something to make of her life. She had no clear idea at the moment where she was going or what she would do. But she had friends in London. Someone would put her up until she found another job. But she sighed as she thought of the weary business of calling at bureaux, and possibly having to work in a dingy office in Town. If only it hadn't been for that affair with Dickon, she might have been happy at 'White Monks'.

Her attention was suddenly recalled to the wheel. About a hundred yards away she saw the silhouette of a man outlined in the middle of the road. He had his arms outstretched and was waving frantically to her to stop.

Judy had a moment's indecision. It might be someone in need of help, in which case she should stop and do what she could, or it might possibly be a trap. Perhaps it would be safer to accelerate and get past as quickly as she could. There was very little traffic on the road at this hour, and if it was by any chance a 'hold-up', there was not much chance of anyone coming by.

Then as she drew nearer, still undecided what to do, with a sudden shock she recognised the man in the road. Edward Traill! And she noticed simultaneously that a large sports car lay on its side in the ditch. Major Traill had obviously had a smash on his way home from the dance. She pulled up 'Muggins' and called out to the Major.

'What's happened? Are you all right?'

He was very pale and shaken, but he looked at Judy in amazement.

'Good lord, what on earth are *you* doing here?'

'Never mind that,' she interrupted. 'The thing is, are you hurt? Can I drive you home?'

'No, I'm all right,' he said. 'Only a bruised shoulder — but Amanda . . . '

Judy's heart missed a beat. She put a hand to her throat.

'*Amanda!*' she repeated. 'Is *she* with you?'

Major Traill was much too worried to wonder what this girl would think of him for keeping Amanda out at this hour. He said:

'Yes. We went for a drive after the dance. We hit the grass verge, I think — I must have gone to sleep at the wheel — Amanda's unconscious — I think she's struck her head — it may be concussion . . . '

Judy jumped out into the road while he was still speaking.

'Where is she?' she asked.

'Over here.'

He led her to the side of the road. Amanda lay on the grass where he had carried her after the accident. Her face was white, and blood oozed from a cut on her forehead. The creamy gardenias that she had worn round her head at the dance were crushed and bruised against her dishevelled hair. Her lips were slightly parted, and as Judy bent over her, Amanda murmured:

'Eddy! Oh, Eddy!'

Immediately the man was on one knee beside her, Judy completely forgotten for the moment.

'What is it, my darling?'

But Amanda had relapsed into unconsciousness again.

Judy spoke abruptly:

'I'll drive back and fetch Ricky. He'll bring the big car. We can't take her in mine — it's too small and bumpy.'

'Be as quick as you can,' Traill urged her. 'Amanda may be seriously hurt.'

Judy felt suddenly sorry for him. He looked so forlorn and anxious, and was obviously badly shaken.

'It's probably not very serious,' she tried to reassure him. 'Mandy'll be all right when we get her to bed. I'll be back as soon as I possibly can. Better put a rug over her; I'll give you one out of my car.'

She fetched the rug and handed it to him. Then she got into the car, turned round, and drove, flat out, towards 'White Monks'.

8

After the dance was over and all the guests had gone, Ricky Portal had not felt inclined for bed. He had too much to think about. Like Judy had done, he sat alone in his room, living again the bitter-sweet memories of the evening. And his heart sank when he contemplated the future — without Judy. She had told him that she intended to leave at once. It had been bad enough having her here and not being able to tell her of the vital urgent love in his heart — but it would be a hundred times worse once she had gone, and he would not even have the happiness of seeing her about the house.

And what of Amanda? Seeing her in the other man's arms tonight had disgusted Ricky. He knew, too, that she had gone out with him in his car after the dance. He had seen them leaving together after everyone else had gone, and had heard Traill's car driving off.

Ricky decided that he must have some exercise. If he tired himself physically, perhaps he would feel more like sleep later. So he changed into his bathing shorts and bath-gown and went down to the swimming-pool. After twenty minutes in the clear, moonlit water, he felt refreshed and in a better frame of mind. He put on his bath-gown again and made his way back to the house.

As he neared the front door, he heard the sound of a car in the drive. The thought that it might be Amanda coming home was soon dispelled. Ricky stood on the front doorstep, rubbing his wet hair with a towel, and waited for the car to appear. Who the devil could it be?

He was utterly astonished when the dear familiar 'Muggins' came into sight.

Judy jumped out of the car and ran to him.

'Oh, Dickon!' she cried. 'Dickon, get

the big car and come quickly.'

'What is it, Judy? What's happened? And why are you out at this hour?'

'I'll explain later,' she said. 'It's Amanda. She was out with Major Traill — and there's been an accident.'

'An accident!' he repeated. 'Is she badly hurt?'

'I don't know,' said Judy. 'She's unconscious. Major Traill is with her now.'

'I'll come right away,' he said. 'Ring for a doctor, my dear, and tell one of the servants to get everything ready in Amanda's room while I dress. I won't be two minutes. We'll take the Bentley and fetch her.'

As she hurried away to do as he asked, she could not help admiring the way he handled the situation. No unnecessary questioning or panic — just a cool head and common-sense. A man like Dickon brought with him a feeling of security.

A few minutes later, as they drove quickly towards the scene of the accident, she explained to him how it was that she had been out at that time of night — her sudden decision to leave then and there, get to London, and hunt for a job.

She realised now, of course, that she wouldn't be able to leave. She must make certain that Amanda was all right. If she was to be laid up, she would want her, Judy, to run the house. And so, thought Judy, she seemed fated to remain at 'White Monks' and see Dickon continually.

Travelling at high speed, they soon reached the spot where Traill's car was lying overturned in the ditch. Dickon leapt out and, ignoring Traill completely, picked his wife up and laid her on the back seat of the car.

Amanda was still unconscious. Edward Traill, who was looking rather abashed and had nothing to say, took his place in the front seat. Judy sat beside her cousin.

They were a silent quartette on the way back. The only sound above the purr of the engine was a moan now and then from Amanda, who was beginning to revive in the open car. An occasional sigh of 'Oh, Eddy — Eddy!' which made Dickon purse his lips.

When they reached 'White Monks', Dickon carried Amanda upstairs and laid her on the bed in her own room. The whole house was now ablaze with lights. All the servants were awake, and there was great activity.

Dickon offered to send Traill home in the Bentley, and gave the chauffeur orders, while Judy sat by Amanda's bedside, watching in case she should recover consciousness.

Then Dr. Martin arrived. Judy had seen him several times before. He quite often came as a guest to 'White Monks'. He had been at the dance; she had thought him a good-looking man.

Judy also thought how like Amanda it was, to have a young, attractive doctor attend her when she was ill.

Martin was efficient and business-like in the sickroom, and Judy was kept busy for the next half hour, helping him.

He discovered that Amanda's right leg was broken and had to be set. The head injuries were not serious, he said. She would soon recover from the effects of the concussion. But her leg would keep her laid up for some time.

When that summer morning came, it found 'White Monks' very much subdued. The lovely young mistress, having had her leg put in a splint, lay asleep under the influence of dope. Judy, who had not left her, still sat at her side, waiting for her to wake. Ricky wandered like a lost soul round the house, gloomily watching the servants take away the debris of last night's ball, and restore order.

Even if Judy had contemplated leaving, in spite of Amanda's accident, that wish was frustrated by Amanda herself.

The moment she wakened from the effects of the dope, she clung to Judy and begged her to stay.

'You're the only person I want with me, Judy. Don't let them bring any hospital nurses to the place. I loathe nurses and all the paraphernalia of sick nursing. It's too depressing. If I've got to be laid up with this leg, you must look after me, darling.'

Judy hesitated a moment.

Last night, after Dickon had kissed her, she had come to a definite conclusion that she must go away at once, whether she had another job or not. The situation was too intolerable. Amanda saw her hesitation and said:

'Don't you *want* to stay with me, Judy?'

Judy coloured and answered:

'Yes, yes, of course.'

'Dr. Martin told me he was sure you could manage. You were so splendid last night.'

'I like nursing,' muttered Judy. 'But . . .'

'What?' asked Amanda, then gave a little moan: 'Oh, how my leg hurts!'

Of course that cry and the sight of

the dark shadows under Amanda's lovely eyes were sufficient to make Judy put aside her own personal troubles and miseries.

'I won't leave you,' she said, patting Amanda's hand. 'If my nursing's good enough, I'll be here when you want me, darling.'

Then, soon afterwards, when Amanda was more comfortable and sleeping again, Judy had a bath, changed into a linen dress and went out into the garden. Her head ached and she was tired. She needed fresh air and some sunshine. There had been all the work and excitement of the ball yesterday, added to which she had had no rest at all last night.

She felt heavy-eyed and depressed. It was not that she minded nursing Amanda. She liked that. And she was flattered by Amanda's preference for her. But it meant that she must go on seeing Dickon. It was so hard to see him day after day and not give way to human weakness — her love which increased rather than diminished.

She met Dickon in the grounds, coming up from the stables after his morning ride. He, too, looked tired, but a gallop in the sunshine had brought back his colour.

The sight of Judy's fatigued, forlorn young face moved him, as always, to tenderness.

'You look as though you want some sleep, you poor child.'

'Oh, I'm fine,' she said, and fingered her belt nervously.

'How's Amanda now?'

'Asleep. She had an hour of rather bad pain. I wonder how long it will take for that leg to get right.'

'A month to six weeks.'

'Oh dear!' said Judy in dismay.

Dickon tapped a riding-crop against his leather boot. He frowned.

'Has Amanda asked you to stay and nurse her?'

'Yes. She seems to want me with her. Of course she doesn't realise that I intended to leave.'

'Well, if you can't, I must.'

'It seems a bit hard, driving you out of your own home,' said Judy miserably.

'It isn't much home to me, my dear, as things are. You know that.'

'But you love 'White Monks'.'

'The place, yes. But the atmosphere — no! Good God! Even when she's half-conscious, she calls for that other fellow.'

Judy made a gesture of hopelessness.

'Why do you allow it?'

'You know why. We agreed to lead our own lives. And as she doesn't love me any more, I can't force her to — even if I wanted to. And I don't. *You* know that.'

He was looking her in the eyes now, and she felt as she always did when Dickon looked at her thus — the maddest desire to give way to all the emotions which she was keeping cooped up inside her. Dickon added:

'I've made so many mistakes in life, Judy. And one of the biggest was when I imagined that the sort of feeling

Amanda and I had for each other in the first place was — love. I know now that it was merely physical infatuation. It died very quickly. The second mistake I made was when I thought we could go our ways and yet share the same house and make some kind of show of it. But that hasn't worked either. It never could work. Marriage was meant for love, companionship, and — most of all — fidelity. It isn't that I'm jealous of Traill. Jealousy doesn't come into it, because I don't love Amanda any more. But it's a sense of what's right and wrong. And you've taught me — what's right!'

'Oh, Dickon,' said Judy, 'I'd give my life to be able to help both of you.'

'The best thing I can do is to go right away,' he said sombrely, 'abroad somewhere.'

She made no reply. But she reflected, wretchedly, that that would mean she would never see him again. It would be so easy to argue herself into believing that because Amanda behaved the way she did, Dickon had a right to behave that way, too. Dickon would have a right to take her, Judy, with him when he went. Yet she could never really believe that either of them should behave that way. She could never be happy, being a party to it.

He seemed to read her thoughts. He gave a sudden smile and laid a hand on her shoulder.

'Don't worry, Judy, I'm not going to ask you to come too. That subject is taboo between us. This travesty of a marriage must go on. But there won't be any other woman in my life — that I'll promise you.'

Her eyes filled with tears. He saw them glittering on her lashes. He turned quickly away.

'For God's sake, don't cry. I couldn't stand that.'

'I'm not crying.'

'Yes, you are.'

'You're an awful arguer,' she said, and turned from him and blew her nose violently.

'I wish I had the chance of a few more arguments with you, my sweet.'

There came a voice from the terrace: 'Miss — Gr-a-ant.'

'That's Ellis calling me. Amanda may want me.'

'Poor Amanda. I hope she won't have too much pain. Look after her, Judy — and after yourself.'

'And you must look after *yourself*,' she said, her eyes suspiciously bright again, then turned and walked quickly down the pathway, leaving him standing there.

9

When Judy entered her cousin's bedroom, she found her in tears.

She went quickly to the bedside.

'Oh, Amanda darling, is it the pain again?'

But Amanda was not weeping with pain. In her hand she held a piece of notepaper, the contents of which she had just read. And Judy remembered with a shock that in the midst of all the excitement she had completely forgotten the letter she had written to Amanda before running away from 'White Monks'. Of course it had been taken up to the mistress of the house with the rest of her letters. What a fool she had been, thought Judy, to have forgotten. What on earth was she going to say to Amanda, and how was she to explain why she had intended leaving her?

Amanda spoke to her cousin in a voice half bitter, half unhappy.

'So you don't like being in my home. You don't much like me. You were walking out on me, and you promised you wouldn't leave me, Judy. You know I don't want anyone but you to look after me. And that's all you care!'

Judy sat on the edge of the bed, and tried to make her explanation.

'It's all right, darling, I won't go, I promise you. I wrote that note before your accident. I did intend to go, I admit, but I won't now. At least, not until you are much better.'

'But why go at all? I thought you were happy here. You must have some reason for leaving — and without even talking things over. What's happened? Has somebody upset you? Can't you get on with the staff — or what?'

Judy sought in her mind, hopelessly, for a satisfactory answer.

'It isn't exactly that I don't like it here, Amanda darling. I — I just don't think it suits me, that's all.'

'Your health, do you mean?'

'No.'

'Then why were you going without telling me — why didn't you wait to see me about it?'

Judy found no answer to that question.

'Amanda, I can't really explain,' she said at length. 'But — I just wanted to go back to Town. I had quite made up my mind to go, and I didn't see much point in staying till morning . . . ' She broke off, acutely conscious that she could hardly have thought of anything more feeble.

Amanda stared at her. Her lovely face was flushed and resentful now.

'My dear child, you don't mean to say that you intended to go off in the middle of the night? You must have taken an inordinate dislike to me, if that's the case.'

'But it isn't. I'm very fond of you, Mandy.'

'Yet you wanted to quit at a moment's notice.'

'Yes,' said Judy, by now thoroughly embarrassed. 'It must sound awfully stupid to you, Amanda, but I just felt I couldn't stay any longer, and so I wrote that note to you and got out the car and — just went!'

'How do you mean, you *went*?' repeated Amanda, mystified. 'How did you know about my accident?'

'I happened to go along the same road, and I found you and Major Traill, and the car on its side in the ditch.'

'Then it was you who fetched Ricky?'

Judy nodded.

'Well, I can't say I understand. You're most mysterious,' said Amanda. 'It's maddening enough to be laid up for weeks with this leg, but if you'd gone, I don't know what I'd have done. Now, be a good child, Judy, and promise me you won't do anything so silly again. And even though you won't explain things, perhaps you'll tell me if there's anything I can do to make you like it better down here.'

Judy murmured her thanks. She

assured Amanda that there was nothing that she could do.

'You get enough time off, don't you?' Amanda continued. 'You can always go out when you wish, as you know, Judy. And if you've got a boyfriend who would like to take you out, for heaven's sake go, or ask him here. I won't mind.'

'I haven't a boyfriend,' Judy said, and got up and walked to the window, anxious that Amanda should not see the colour that rose to her cheeks.

'As a matter of fact, my dear, I believe Dr. Martin is rather intrigued with you,' added Amanda. 'I noticed last night he made a bee-line for you at the beginning of the first dance. He's a nice soul, and really quite worth encouraging. You might do worse, darling.'

Judy had flushed to the roots of her hair. She knew perfectly well that Amanda wouldn't care how many 'boyfriends' she went out with. And she was quite aware that Dr. Martin had taken more than an ordinary amount of notice of her last night, before Dickon had managed to get away from his 'duty dances' and join her. But Judy didn't want any attention from any man. She was in love with the one person whom she must not love. Amanda's husband! If Amanda but knew!

Too embarrassed to say anything more to Amanda, Judy murmured an excuse and walked out of the room.

That same afternoon, Richard Portal went away.

Judy did not see him go. She presumed that he shied from a parting scene with her. And although she hated the knowledge that he had left 'White Monks', it meant that the strain was lifted from her a little, since she must stay here with Amanda.

She had plenty to do, because the spoiled Amanda hardly allowed her to leave her side, except when Traill, or some of her most amusing friends, called to see her. Her boudoir and bedroom were filled with flowers, books, and magazines. The telephone rang all day with messages and inquiries.

And the more that Judy did for Amanda, the more difficult she felt that it would be to leave her. Amanda kept repeating that she must never, never go away from 'White Monks'. She seemed so genuinely grateful to Judy for her tireless and efficient nursing.

And inevitably Judy was brought into contact frequently with Amanda's physician.

For the first week or so, Hugh Martin came almost every day to attend to Amanda's leg. It was giving some slight trouble, but even when that settled down, he began, on invitation from Amanda, to drop in on purely friendly visits at cocktail time.

It was obvious to Amanda that he was attracted by her young cousin, and with the instincts of a matchmaker, she did everything she could to encourage the affair. But Judy remained disinterested. She refused several invitations from him to take her out to dinner or a show in Oxford. She gave him no encouragement.

Amanda, growing fit and strong again herself, felt it was time to have a straight talk with her cousin on the subject of marriage. She opened the conversation one morning when she was lying in bed propped up by pillows, with a tray in front of her. Judy usually came in to talk to her while she had her breakfast.

'Darling,' Amanda said casually, 'why don't you take any notice of Hugh Martin? He came in here yesterday looking most depressed, and after a little discreet questioning on my part, I discovered that *you* are the cause of all the gloom.'

'Oh!' said Judy. 'Why?'

'Well, he's afraid he's offended you, because you won't take any notice of him, and refuse to go out with him.'

'There's no question of my being offended. I just don't want to go out with him.'

'But why, darling? Don't you like

him? I think he's so sweet! In fact, I'm rather inclined to be jealous that he pays so much more attention to you than to poor little Mandy.' She lapsed into baby talk, and looked at Judy through her long, pretty lashes.

Judy thought:

'Love — love affairs are the breath of life to Mandy. She could flirt with anybody. Why can't I feel that way? Why must I think always of the *one* man?'

'Yes, I like Dr. Martin,' at length she admitted. He seemed an extremely nice man, and she would have liked to have had him for a friend. But she fully realised that he was interested in her in a different way. She could tell that from the way he looked at her, and from the odd little remarks that he made, that he was in love with her. And she didn't want any man for a lover. She didn't want anyone but Dickon, and as she couldn't have him, no one else would do in his place.

'Well, I think you might do well to cultivate Hugh,' Amanda was saying.

'Besides being amusing, he isn't badly off, you know.' Then she added casually: 'By the way, I heard from Ricky this morning.'

Judy's heart beat suddenly a little quicker. Hugh was immediately forgotten again. The only news she received of Dickon was when he wrote to Amanda. She knew he was in Cannes with friends. But although he had been away several weeks now, she still felt a throb of pain at the mention of him, which proved that it was going to be much harder than she had ever believed, to blot out the memory of love and of that first long kiss which had laid upon her lips; that kiss which had bred in her such a deathless passion.

'How is he?' She tried to keep the eagerness out of her voice.

'Oh, very fit,' said Amanda. 'Having a marvellous time — bathing and dancing and rushing round the casinos, and all the rest of it.'

'Oh, is he?' Judy said in the same

politely interested tone, although actually she longed to demand to be shown the letter and read it for herself. Read every word exactly as he had written it.

'I heard from another friend of mine in Cannes yesterday,' continued Amanda. 'She says that Phyll Redding is there at the moment.'

'Who is Phyll Redding?' Judy asked.

Amanda enlightened her. Phyll was one of the last year's débutantes, and was considered one of the loveliest girls in London. All the men were mad about her. Ricky, she thought, also had a slight penchant for Phyll.

Judy received this news in silence. She tried not to feel jealous. Hadn't Dickon told her that there would never be 'another woman'? On the other hand, if he was out there in a party, why should he remain aloof? He would be bound, if only for courtesy's sake, to join in and do as the others did. Even if he hated every moment of it, he would have to 'bathe, dance and rush round the casinos with beautiful débutantes.'

She tried to reassure herself. But at the same time there came a most disturbing mental picture of Dickon acting as escort to 'one of the loveliest girls in London.'

She got up from the bed abruptly and, making the excuse that she had some work in the house to do, walked to the door.

'Darling!' Amanda called after her. 'You *will* try to be nice to poor Hugh, won't you? He's such a lamb, and he'd be so thrilled if you'd take just a *tiny* bit of notice of him now and then.'

Judy half smiled.

'All right, I'll try,' she said.

As she walked along the corridor, Judy argued half apologetically with herself that it was foolish to continue to avoid Dr. Martin, just because she could not like him otherwise than as a friend. Anyway, she could not spend the rest of her life refusing invitations because of her hopeless passion for Dickon.

She felt almost disloyal to him

because she had told Amanda she would 'be nice' to Hugh Martin. But after all, she told herself, Dickon was going out and about, whether he enjoyed it or not, and she would go out, too, and see if she could extract any pleasure from life in the companionship of Hugh Martin. Why not accept the next invitation he made to her?

Amanda meanwhile settled herself back on her pillows, congratulating herself that she had helped to build up a little 'local interest' for Judy which would, she hoped, remove from her all desire to leave 'White Monks'.

10

A few days after her conversation with Amanda, Dr. Martin asked Judy to go with him to a play in Oxford, which the O.U.D.S. were presenting.

'I know most of the fellows,' the young doctor told her. 'And if it will amuse you, we will go round and look them up after the show.'

Judy accepted the invitation, although she did not feel much enthusiasm. But that was what she told herself she must overcome — this apathetic frame of mind and indifference to life unless Dickon was there. She would put her love for Dickon on one side, and resign herself to the fact that she must not see him again. He would probably be away another fortnight, and before that, Amanda would be better, and she, Judy, would be free to leave 'White Monks' and make a new start. She would resolutely put the past behind her.

When Amanda heard that Judy was going out with Hugh, she smiled to herself. She imagined that her talk had had the desired effect. And she secretly hoped that Judy would have 'a nice little affair' with the young doctor. It might even end in marriage. Amanda was sincerely fond of Judy these days. She would like the funny little thing to 'get a kick out of life'.

She said as much to Edward Traill one evening about a week later, when he came to see her.

'You know, Eddy, it just saved the situation, Hugh turning up when he did with a 'grande passion' for Judy.'

Edward took a puff of the cigarette he was smoking and blew three successive smoke-rings into the air.

'In what way has it saved the situation, my sweet?'

'Well, Judy seemed to be getting a little unsettled, and talked a lot of rot about it not suiting her here, and wanting to leave. In fact, Eddy, if it hadn't been for the accident, she would have left that night. That was why it was she who found us smashed up — she was clearing out.'

'I wondered several times why Judy should have been out at that hour,' replied Traill. 'But what was her reason for leaving in the middle of the night?'

Amanda shrugged her shoulders.

'Lord knows! I couldn't get much out of her. Anyway, I persuaded her to stay until I was better. But now that the Doc's interested in her, I'm hoping she may change her mind and decide to stay on altogether.'

'Quite likely, I should imagine,' said Edward, not particularly interested in Judy. 'She's a useful young woman, I suppose.'

'Quite indispensable, darling,' was Amanda's reply, accompanied by a dazzling smile. 'She takes all the nasty horrid work off little Mandy's shoulders, and leaves her more time for her Edward.'

Traill regained interest. He understood baby talk from Amanda and knew how to react to it.

'Then, lady mine, I can only hope that the cousin finds her doctor friend so absorbing that she will never again contemplate leaving little Mandy's Monkey House.'

Amanda gave a delighted gurgle.

'Dar-*ling*, what a gorgeous name for it. But don't let Ricky hear you call it that. He's so very proud of it.'

'Ricky won't be home yet awhile. And before he comes back, I hope to have persuaded little Mandy to run away with her Eddy.'

But Amanda shook her head and grew serious again.

'No, Eddy, I can't. It's so complicated. You see, it isn't only Ricky — there are so many things . . . ' She broke off delicately, forbearing to give the true explanation of the 'complications,' which was that Edward's income was not as large as Ricky's.

'Well, you know that if ever you

change your mind, I'll be ready to take you,' said Traill.

Amanda sighed.

'If only things were as easy for us as they are for Judy and Hugh,' she said.

But had Amanda known it, Judy and Hugh were finding things anything but 'easy'.

The first two or three outings Judy had had with Hugh had passed off quite well. He had given no sign that he wished the affair to be on more than a platonic basis, and Judy had begun to feel quite at home with him, and, indeed, to enjoy his company She even tried to harden her heart against thoughts of Dickon. And it was some slight consolation to her to be out with Hugh now that she knew that Dickon was 'rushing round Cannes' with girls like Phyll Redding, spending his evenings dancing, or gambling at the casino.

Not that she thought Dickon was really attracted by Phyll or anyone else. He had told her that he would never care for another woman, and she had implicit faith in him in that respect. But still, if he had decided that it was no good to sit down and brood over the tragedy of their love, then she would follow his example.

But that wasn't quite the kind of foundation for a happy love affair with Hugh.

In fact, Judy was in no mood for a love affair with anyone. Hugh was a dear — good-looking, debonair, a promising young physician. But she still had the apathetic feeling that she didn't really care what she did or where she went. It was a matter of unimportance to her whether Hugh took her to dinner or to a theatre, or whether they just stayed at 'White Monks', and turned on the wireless or talked. She liked his being there, because it prevented her from thinking too much about Dickon, and he was always nice to her, and an amusing conversationalist.

But she began to realise, as time went on, that sooner or later she would have to face up to the fact that Hugh's feelings for her were not purely platonic. The time would come when she would have to come to some understanding with him. Their pleasant comradeship was bound to end.

There came a lovely summer's night when Hugh Martin took Judy to a dance in Oxford. He was a good dancer, and Judy enjoyed it. But she was a little worried. His easy, friendly manner had changed this evening. He looked at her just a little more intimately than usual, and when they danced he held her just a little more possessively.

She was not altogether surprised, therefore, when on the way home, he suddenly turned off the main road down a quiet side lane, stopped the car and switched off the headlamps.

She nerved herself to cope with what was to come. For some reason she felt just a little apprehensive. She had decided long ago just how much she would tell him when the question did arise, but she was not looking forward to it.

Hugh Martin had turned his head and was regarding her intently, trying to read her thoughts. A faint glimmer of moonlight showed him the outline of her charming face in profile as she stared ahead of her. He was badly in love with this girl who was so utterly different from his lovely society patient, so different, in fact, that it was difficult to realise that they were related.

'Judy,' he said tenderly, moving closer to her and putting an arm around her shoulders.

He felt her body stiffen.

'No, Hugh, *please*!' she said.

'What's the matter?' he asked, as she drew away from him.

'Nothing. I just don't want you to make love to me.'

She felt sorry for him, because she did not want to hurt him.

'Why not?' he asked. 'I want to so much, Judy. I've got rather fond of you, my dear. Why won't you let me kiss you?'

'I don't want you to,' she said in a distressed voice. She *couldn't* let any other man but Dickon kiss her. 'I'm sorry, Hugh, but I don't love you, and I wouldn't let anyone make love to me whom I didn't love.'

This reply irritated Hugh, irritated more than hurt him. She was going to behave like a little Puritan, was she? He leaned back in his seat and gave her a queer, sidelong look.

'You weren't so particular that night at the Checkley Inn, were you, my dear?'

Judy's heart missed a beat. She glanced up at him quickly with wide, frightened eyes.

'What do you mean?'

'What do you think I mean? Don't you remember being rather nicer to Ricky Portal in the Checkley Inn than you are being to me tonight?'

Judy's lips opened, but she made no sound. White and shaken, she sat there, staring before her. How in heaven's name had Hugh found out about *that night*? And having found out, what did he intend to do about it? He might make a great deal of trouble if he wanted to. She stammered:

'How do you know about that . . . tell me how you found out . . . '

Hugh Martin lit himself a cigarette before he answered, because he knew she was waiting impatiently to hear what he had to say. He was rather enjoying this moment. He did not intend to be hoodwinked by any high principles on Judy's part, he told himself. He found her very attractive. He had thought so, from the glimpse he had caught of her that night at the inn, in Ricky Portal's arms. And he had been very astonished when he recognised her at 'White Monks', and had thought privately that Ricky must have manœuvred things so that he could carry on an affair with Judy in his own house, under cover of her job as housekeeper.

He said:

'I happened to be at the inn the same night, Judy. And, if you remember, the door of the lounge was open. I was just walking past. But — er — I think you were too busy at the time to notice me.'

Judy's cheeks flamed. She put both hands up to them. She was feeling embarrassed and quite a little frightened. Of course Hugh had seen Dickon kissing her! It was certainly the most unfortunate coincidence that he should happen to be at the inn that particular night.

'Why didn't you tell me this before?' she asked.

He shrugged his shoulders.

'There wasn't much point in making trouble. Besides, I was afraid that if I told Amanda, she might send you away, and I thought you rather too attractive to risk that happening.'

She objected to his tone of voice, and in fact his whole demeanour. He was totally unlike his usual quiet, charming self. She thought how completely and hideously a man could change in a moment of frustrated passion. She had no idea he could be so horrible. She said, coldly:

'I'm afraid you're wasting your time if you think I am at all interested in your opinion of me. I'm not the least bit in love with you. And, as to what you saw at the inn — I suppose there was no harm in my having some supper with Ricky?'

'None at all, my dear. But it's one things to have supper with a man, and quite another, kissing him quite so ardently as you were doing, especially when he happens to be married.'

Judy stayed silent again. So he *had* seen Dickon kiss her! Well, he was obviously out to be unpleasant about it. She floundered in her mind for something to say. She did not know how to deal with this man. At length she said:

'Hugh, don't you think you could try to forget what you saw that night? I assure you I haven't been carrying on an affair with Ricky behind Amanda's back, if that's what you imagine. And it can do no good bringing that episode into the light now. You don't understand the circumstances.'

'I understand enough to know that you spent that night at the inn with Ricky, and that you've both been living under the same roof ever since,' he said.

Judy turned on him in a fury.

'You've no right to say that. It isn't true. I didn't spend the night with Ricky. How can you say such a thing? You're despicable!'

He patted her arm.

'Don't lose your temper, my dear,' he said. 'Whether you spent the night together or not is open to doubt, but that doesn't alter the fact that I saw you in Ricky's arms.'

'But, Hugh, you don't understand. My car had broken down and Ricky gave me a lift, and as it was late and the weather was bad, we put up at the inn. I was starting work at 'White Monks' the next day, and I'd never even met him before . . . '

'That makes it all the worse,' he put in dryly.

'Let me finish,' she retorted with spirit. 'We had supper, and talked. Then somehow we both found we were in love with each other — we couldn't help it. I admit he kissed me. Then I went up to bed, but Ricky got the car out and drove away.'

'Love at first sight, and then — the grand renunciation!' Hugh remarked with sarcasm.

'Can't you *try* to understand?' she said, exasperated. 'Ricky was only trying to do the right thing. He left a note for me which I got in the morning. I thought I'd never see him again. But it wasn't till I got to 'White Monks' the next day that I found he was Amanda's husband. If you'd any real feeling, you'd realise that it was a pretty intolerable position.'

'I should have said it was quite the opposite,' he said in the same sneering sarcastic voice. 'You and Ricky in the same house — Amanda all unsuspecting. What opportunities you must have had!'

Judy was so angry she could not speak for a moment. Then she said in an ice-cold voice:

'I'm not going to argue with you any more. The only thing I ask is, if you have any decency in you, you will not tell Amanda what you saw at the Checkley. She might put the same construction on it that you have done, and that is entirely wrong. Now, will you please take me home at once.'

The man smoked his cigarette thoughtfully. He knew that he was behaving like a cad, but he was not in the mood for renunciation himself, nor anything but thwarted and annoyed because he imagined that this girl had been carrying on an affair with Ricky Portal. What right had she to become so prudish where he, Hugh, was concerned? He had been patient and careful with Judy since he first took her out, because he had known that she was a difficult, sensitive person, and would not react well to his love-making if he hurried things. But now those tactics had failed, he decided to try firmer methods.

'Before I take you home,' he said, 'we must have the position quite clear. Do I understand that you object to me because your feelings for Ricky are serious?'

'I've told you, I'm in love with him.'

'But surely, if things are as much in earnest as this, you have no right to ask me to promise not to let his wife know about it. She ought to know. And I'm one of her pals.'

'Hugh, for heaven's sake, be reasonable,' said Judy. 'I can't help being in love with Ricky, but I've given you my word that we're not doing anything about it. And anyway, I'm going away before Ricky comes back. You can do no possible good by telling Amanda.'

'Then, my dear,' he said, 'if you've put this affair behind you, surely it would be a good idea to give me a chance, and see if I can't help you to forget your troubles.'

'I don't want anyone to help me forget — like that,' Judy said. 'And will you *please* drive me home.'

'Then,' he said, ignoring her request, 'if you don't want anyone to help you forget, how do you expect me to believe that you want to end things with Ricky?'

'You'll have to take my word for it.'

'Why not prove that, by being a little kinder to me, and showing me that you mean it.'

Judy began an angry retort, but he cut her short.

'What it comes down to is this. If you'll let me take you out sometimes and give you a good time, but on a *slightly* more friendly basis than before' — he gave her a meaning look — 'I shall take it for granted that you mean to finish things with Ricky. But if not — then I shall be forced to the conclusion that you still intend to see him when he comes back, and I shall feel it my duty to tell Amanda.'

Judy was speechless. This was nothing short of blackmail. While she was still searching in her mind for something to say in answer to him, he suddenly switched on the engine, started the car, and turned it round, heading for 'White Monks'.

'I should think it over, my dear,' he added, 'and let me know what you decide to do.'

11

Judy entered Amanda's bedroom the next morning, fully prepared to tell her that she intended to leave in a week's time.

The scene with Hugh had distressed her greatly, not only because she had discovered that he had known all along about that episode in the Checkley Inn, but because he had shown himself to be such an utter cad. She was somewhat shocked to think that anyone who had appeared so charming could possibly have that side to his character.

After Hugh had left her and she was in her room, she had decided that she could not stay at 'White Monks', knowing that at any moment Hugh might give her away to Amanda. For she, hearing his side of the story, might easily put the worst construction on it. Much better to leave as soon as she could. After all, she would be going very soon, anyway. She did not know when Ricky was coming back, but he had already been away over a month. Amanda did not really need her now. She was getting about well on her crutches and probably in another week or so she would be almost all right again. She had plenty of visitors. The usual round of cocktail parties had begun again, and the strains of dance music on radio and gramophone filled the house.

Judy found Amanda sitting up in bed, looking through a pile of letters. As she seated herself on the edge of the bed, she noticed a thin foreign envelope, about half-way down the pile, bearing a French stamp. From Dickon! Judy could hardly conceal her impatience for Amanda to open it and tell her the news. But Amanda, in her usual leisurely way, was taking her time with her mail, tearing open one envelope, reading out any bits she thought would be of interest to Judy, then reminiscing on any incident that the writer of the letter recalled to her mind, and finally throwing it aside and attacking the next one in the same way.

At last the foreign envelope with the French stamp appeared on top and was torn open.

Amanda skimmed through the contents carelessly, as if they were of little or no interest to her. The she pushed the letter back into its envelope, remarking casually:

'Ricky still seems to be painting the French coast red. He says they're at Dinard now. I prefer Cannes myself, but I suppose so long as there's a casino, they'll find life bearable.'

Judy avoided her cousin's gaze.

'Does Ricky say when he's coming back?' she ventured to ask, her heart-beats quickening as they still did whenever she mentioned or heard that name.

'Oh yes — he mentions it somewhere.' Amanda took the letter out again and glanced at it. 'Let's see

— where was it — oh yes, here we are! He's arriving next Wednesday and hopes to get here in time for dinner.'

Judy stayed silent. But her heartbeats were faster than ever. If Dickon were coming back so soon, it gave her a double reason for telling Amanda that she wished to leave. She would have to try to find somebody else to take her place as housekeeper. Judy had decided to tell Amanda first that she had been offered another job, and secondly that she did not feel well at 'White Monks'. Two excuses for leaving. Whatever she did, she must lie, since she could not possibly tell the truth.

Amanda was chatting blithely about an incident that had occurred the last time she was in Dinard. Judy listened vaguely, putting in a comment here and there. She mustn't broach the subject of her departure right on top of the news of Dickon's expected return, otherwise Amanda would surely start putting two and two together.

Eventually she managed to lead the

conversation round to Amanda's injured leg.

'You'll soon be allowed to walk without your crutches, won't you, darling?' she asked.

'Yes. Hughie thinks I can discard them for a little bit each day after this week. Isn't it marvellous! It'll be so lovely to get round again without those damn sticks. Darling, they aren't exactly *becoming*, are they?'

Judy weighed in.

'The thing is, Amanda, if you're really well enough to look after yourself again, I shall be free to leave, as I intended.'

Amanda stared at her cousin.

'Judy, you're not going to start all *that* again!'

'But, Amanda, it was decided that I should only stay until you were better. We left it like that.'

'But I thought you were happier here now. I hoped you wouldn't want to go.'

Judy looked away uncomfortably.

'I'm sorry, but I'd honestly rather, if

you don't mind.'

'But it's absurd!' protested Amanda. 'You can have no earthly excuse for wanting to leave.'

Up shot Judy's brown head.

'I must be allowed to choose my own life.'

Amanda was truly astonished.

'Of course, darling, I know. But I don't understand why you don't like it here.'

'Oh, I do, in a way,' broke in Judy. 'But on the whole, I think I'd be better in Town, that's all. Besides — I've been offered another job.'

Lie number one. That didn't go over too badly, she thought. It sounded quite plausible.

'Oh, is that it?' Amanda sounded relieved. 'What sort of job is it? Has someone offered you a bigger salary or something? Because, you know, I wouldn't quibble about giving you as much as anyone else offers, if I could keep you here.'

'No, it's not a question of money,

Amanda. I just think I shall like it better, that's all.'

'But what sort of job is it?'

'Oh — secretarial. Secretary to an M.P. or something.'

'What's his name?'

'I can't remember offhand.' Judy tried to sound convincing. 'It's no use arguing about it, Amanda. I've made up my mind.'

Amanda, spoiled and pampered, began to be argumentative.

'I honestly don't see why. I mean, even supposing I'd been a tartar and overworked you, been too casual with you, or something — what about Hugh Martin? I thought you and he were getting on so well. I hoped you'd want to stay here. You do like Hugh, don't you?'

Judy hesitated. Actually at this moment there was no one in the world whom she disliked more thoroughly. But she could not tell Amanda that.

'I can't let Hugh or anyone else stand in the way of a good job.'

'Nonsense, darling; if you were *really* in love with him, you wouldn't want to take a job away from here,' Amanda said sharply, irritated by what she felt was a display of stubborn stupidity on her young cousin's part.

Judy felt irritated in her turn. Why should Amanda jump to the conclusion that because Hugh had taken her out once or twice, she was in love with him. What did Amanda know about being in love? Amanda whose love for any man was always overshadowed by the size of his banking account.

'Probably not,' she replied a little dryly. 'But as it happens I don't pretend to be *really* in love with Hugh. As a matter of fact, I'm not the least bit in love with him.'

'But, *darling!*' said Amanda, 'surely you and Hugh aren't going all platonic? If you were nice to him, I'm sure he'd respond.'

'Perhaps I don't want him to,' said Judy rather sharply. 'I've told you, Amanda, I'm not in love with him, and

I'm not going to let him influence my decision to take another job.'

Amanda did her best to plead with Judy. She was really quite upset at the thought of losing her cousin. She had been so very useful, and the house had run on oiled wheels since she came. Judy did not bother her with any details. And so unobtrusive was she, so easy to get on with, that it had all been a huge success from Amanda's point of view. Added to which, since Dr. Martin had appeared on the scene and fallen in love with Judy, Amanda had honestly believed that his continual visits to the house would be sufficient to keep Judy here.

Judy knew what Amanda was thinking, and felt angry with her. Amanda was so short-sighted. So long as things were easy for her in this life, she did not bother to find out whether they were right for anybody else. So long as everything seemed all right on the surface, she would never take the trouble to probe underneath and get to the bottom of things. It was her selfishness again. That incurable 'ego' which had ruined Dickon and their married life.

Amanda argued, questioned, pleaded. She pointed out how lost she would be without Judy, told her that she wasn't really strong enough to have all the extra work on her shoulders just yet.

But Judy was firm. She would, she said, give her a week to get someone else. In fact, she would do her best during that time to find someone who could take her place.

'It isn't by any chance because of Ricky that you want to go, is it, Judy?' Amanda asked suddenly. 'I mean, he hasn't been beastly to you at any time, or anything — made you feel unwelcome? He doesn't mean it, you know. He's very quiet by nature . . .'

Judy, feeling her face grow red, then white, broke in:

'No, no, of course it isn't that, Amanda. Ricky has never been — beastly to me.'

'Well, you must wait and see him, anyhow,' said Amanda crossly. 'Otherwise you might hurt his feelings, going just before he comes back. And look here — are you sure I couldn't say something to him — I mean — if I couldn't get Ricky to take you out sometimes when Hugh is busy — would you stay? He can be quite nice when he wishes to.'

That left Judy speechless. Amanda was impossible, and that was too crude. So vivid a scarlet did she blush before she made a hasty exit, that it gave Amanda food for thought. Amanda was no fool. Suddenly she saw light. She thought:

'Heavens! Surely the dear little idiot hasn't fallen for Ricky! Perhaps *that's* why she wants to go. I believe I've hit the mark at last. Poor kid, what a damned shame!'

Following upon the philanthropic pity came a curiosity as to how Ricky really regarded her cousin. He had never shown any particular liking for her. She was so quiet. There was nothing at all dazzling about her. Of course she was charming to look at, but possibly she bored Ricky. Amanda thought:

'I must remember to tell Ricky when he comes home that he's made a conquest. Perhaps if he pays her more attention that might persuade her to stay. I don't want her to feel miserable. I'm sure she's one of those romantic people who take things like that to heart.'

Then she remembered Hugh Martin and of what Judy had told her about their relationship. Characteristically she jumped to the conclusion that the affair was on a purely friendly footing, and that they both felt the same about it. She just supposed, vaguely, that Judy must be one of those girls in whom men confide and choose for their friends, but who possess little or no sex-appeal. She wondered if anyone had ever made love to Judy, how much she knew of the 'grande passion,' and whether she had ever had an 'affair'. But these were fleeting thoughts that soon gave place to other, less speculative ones. She thought of Edward Traill and wondered what he was doing today. She reached out an arm and lifted the receiver from the phone on her bed-table, and rang him up to wish him good morning.

Judy was inclined to congratulate herself that she had, on the whole, come out of the interview with her cousin with some credit. When Amanda's mind was set on a thing, it was not an easy matter to argue with her. And Amanda obviously wanted her own way over the question of whether or not Judy left 'White Monks'.

Judy told herself that the only way to manage Amanda was to stand firm and not give way to her. Amanda had a knack of playing on one's sympathy and making herself appear helpless and in need of support, but if one just realised that it was a pose and did not allow one's pity to be aroused, it was really quite easy to defeat her at her own game.

Certainly Amanda's final remark about Ricky had given Judy a considerable jar. So at last Amanda had been astute enough to connect up her decision to leave with Ricky's return. But fortunately she had jumped to an utterly wrong conclusion, since she supposed that Judy was piqued because of Ricky's casual manner. *Casual* — her Dickon — her love! Amanda was still far off the truth, Judy thought. And she had not the slightest idea that Amanda had even remotely guessed at her real feelings.

She felt a weight lifted from her mind with the knowledge that she had convinced Amanda of her intention to leave, and she was determined to go before Dickon returned. Hard though it would be to leave without seeing him, it would be better than waiting till he came back, see him perhaps for a few hours, and then have to part from him again.

That same evening, about half-past six, Judy was busy putting some freshly picked roses into a vase on the table on the terrace. She had already changed for dinner and was waiting to be called to Amanda's room to help her dress.

Hearing the sound of a car in the drive, Judy glanced up from the flowers to see who was coming. Edward Traill presumably.

But it was not Edward. Judy would have recognised the large black-and-silver Bentley anywhere. Her heart gave a tremendous leap. Dickon's car! But it *couldn't* be Dickon. He wasn't due home for another week.

But as the car drew closer, all doubt faded. It *was* Dickon sitting at the wheel. Dickon, brown and radiant from the Mediterranean sun, wearing a white linen driving coat and helmet.

He drew up at the front door, got out, and mounted the terrace steps two at a time, taking off the helmet as he did so.

'Judy, my dear,' he said, taking her

hands. 'My *dear*! How grand to see you again. I was half afraid I wouldn't find you here.'

'Dickon . . . ' she stammered. 'What are you doing — I mean — why are you back so soon?'

He looked surprised.

'Didn't Amanda get my letter?'

'Only the one telling us to expect you next week.'

'Next week? But there was no question of my coming next week. I wrote last week-end saying I was arriving today. She ought to have got it.'

Judy suddenly saw daylight.

'Oh, I think I see what's happened. Your letter only got here this morning, and when Amanda read that you were coming home 'Next Wednesday' she took it for granted that you meant next week.'

Dickon laughed.

'How stupid of me. I ought to have put the date. Never mind — I expect there'll be something for me to eat, won't there?'

'Yes, of course.' (That was the least of her worries, she thought!)

'How's Mandy?' Dickon asked.

'Much better — she'll soon be walking without crutches.'

'That's fine.'

There was a moment's pause, then Dickon said in a low voice:

'It's so grand to see you again, Judy. I was somehow afraid you might have gone before I came back.'

She was white and shaking with emotion at the sight of him, at the touch of his hands. But she managed to control herself.

'Dickon — I meant to go. I told Amanda this morning that I was going to leave — but I thought you weren't coming back until next week. I intended to go back to London, and get another job and never see you again.'

'Did you want to do that, Judy?' he asked.

'You know I didn't. But what I want to do doesn't come into it. It's what I *must* do that matters. I can't go living

196

in the same house with you — I told you so before you went away.'

'Then you still care for me?'

'Yes,' she said under her breath. 'And that's exactly why I must go.'

'I haven't any right to try to stop you, Judy,' he said, 'however much I want to. But God knows it's going to be hard. I have been away from you a long time — so much too long. And I haven't stopped wanting you for a single hour. Do you know that Dowson poem?'

He began to quote to her softly, his dark handsome eyes drinking in the fresh charm of that young face which was so much more charming than any of the lovely, famous ones which had been before him in the South of France all these weeks.

'I have called for madder music and stronger wine,
Hoping to put thy pale lost lilies out of sight . . .
But when the feast is finished and the lamps expire —

Then falls thy shadow — and the night is thine!'

'Cynara,' she whispered, and her eyes suffused with tears of sheer happiness because he still loved her.

'Cynara,' he nodded. 'And I have been faithful to *thee*, darling — in my fashion.'

'Oh, Dickon!'

They stood looking at each other for a moment, happy because of their meeting, miserable at the thought of the coming parting, still utterly and completely in love. Then Judy said:

'There's another reason why I must go, Dickon.'

'What, darling?'

Judy gave a somewhat disjointed account of last night's scene with Hugh Martin. She explained that she had accepted his invitations to try, as he, Dickon, had done, to find some interest in life. Dickon listened in silence until she told him of Hugh's threat to tell Amanda that he had seen them at the inn unless Judy would respond to his love-making. Then he broke out:

'But, Judy, it's monstrous! I wouldn't have belived he could be such a cad!'

'Nor would I,' she said. 'But I thought the best thing to do would be to clear out, and just hope he thinks better of it.'

'I shall go round and tell him exactly what I think of him.'

'No, don't do that,' said Judy. 'It won't do any good. If he does decide to make mischief, we'll just have to tell Amanda the truth, and hope she'll believe it.'

'I suppose so,' said Dickon. 'It was damn bad luck Martin being at the inn that night, anyhow. But if the worst comes to the worst, we can prove that I didn't stay there.'

'He probably won't say anything,' said Judy, trying to look on the bright side. 'I expect he just felt annoyed last night because I wouldn't let him make love to me. After he's thought things over, he'll realise that he's put the wrong construction on the whole thing.'

'We'll hope you're right,' Dickon said. 'And don't let's worry about it, anyhow.'

He took her arm and walked with her along the terrace and into the house.

12

From the window of her room upstairs Amanda had been watching the little scene between Judy and Ricky. When she heard the car in the drive, she had hobbled to the window to see who was coming. When she had recovered from the surprise of seeing her husband, she took an interest in trying to discover whether Judy's reception of Ricky would confirm her suspicions of this morning.

It did not occur to her for a moment that Ricky, himself, might be the one to give anything away. She had taken it for granted that Judy was suffering from a 'schoolgirl passion' for Ricky. It never once entered her head that he felt the slightest interest in her.

It was doubly a shock to her, therefore, when she saw her husband leap out of his car, mount the terrace steps two at a time, and take both Judy's hands in his, betraying all his rapture at seeing her again.

Amanda could not hear what they said, but there was an expression of tenderness on Ricky's face that had never been there for her, and a light in Judy's eyes which made her suddenly quite beautiful.

And then Amanda realised that this must be a much more serious matter than she had thought at first. It was no mere infatuation on Judy's part only. She and Ricky were truly and definitely in love with each other.

Amanda waited to see no more. She moved to the chaise-longue, sank on to it, and did some hard thinking. And she began to understand a whole lot of things that had been incomprehensible to her before.

She saw now a perfectly clear reason for Judy's attempt to leave in the middle of the night, after the dance. Probably, during the evening, she and Ricky had decided between them that they must not go on seeing each other and that Judy must do the right thing and go away. Since they had obviously not wanted her, Amanda, to know the real reason for Judy's departure, she had been on the point of leaving then and there without any explanation. Then, when Judy had been compelled to stay and look after her, Ricky had presumably decided to go away instead. She had, of course, already guessed that it was on Ricky's account that Judy had determined to leave 'White Monks'.

And of course, if the child really was in love with Ricky, it explained her reluctance to go out with Dr. Martin for the first few weeks after Ricky went away. She had probably got a sort of 'loyalty complex', and thought it would be unfair to Ricky if she allowed another man to take notice of her. Then later, when the first pangs of grief at the parting had worn off, she had realised the futility of breaking her heart over any man, and took what the gods offered, in the form of Hugh's friendship. With her usual lack of perception, Amanda decided that it was lucky for Judy that Hugh was the kind of man who took a girl out because he enjoyed her company, and not on account of any romantic feelings towards her. She felt that Judy was the idealistic sort of person who could not care to carry on an affair with anyone when she was in love with someone else.

Amanda decided that the best thing to do would be to pump Ricky when he came up to see her, try to trip him up, and make doubly sure that her suspicions were well founded. Besides, it would be fun to tease old Ricky and see how he reacted to it.

He came up soon after his meeting with Judy. After they had exchanged casual inquiries as to each other's health, Ricky explained why he was home earlier than he was expected. He congratulated her on being able to get about again, and told her that he had had a good holiday, plenty of sunshine, but too many late nights, and he felt rather tired.

'Had any affairs, darling?' Amanda asked sweetly.

'No,' was Ricky's short reply.

'Women don't seem to amuse you these days.'

'Perhaps they don't.'

Amanda lit a cigarette and reclined gracefully among the white satin cushions on the chaise longue in her bedroom. She wore a black satin cocktail suit, and looked enchantingly fair in it. But Ricky was scarcely conscious of her. He was thinking of Judy and how sweet she had appeared to him just now. How different from the blasé, sophisticated crowd he had been associating with abroad.

Then Amanda said:

'By the way, why don't you be nice and unselfish and take Judy out sometimes — to a show or lunch on the river or something?'

Ricky started as Amanda cut in on his thoughts.

'Why should I?'

'Well, darling, she gave me notice this morning. Said she wanted to go.'

'Well?'

'Well, I don't want to lose her. She's much too useful. Besides, I like her. And I think if you were very nice to her she might stay.'

Richard Portal looked thoroughly startled.

'What *do* you mean, Mandy?'

'Well, darling, you may find her very shy and a bit quiet, but it's really too divine — she's got a crush on you. I believe it's because of you she wants to go. The poor dear just went crimson when I said that you ought to take her out.'

He did not answer for a moment. But Amanda saw two little white lines appear on either side of his mouth. Lines that her experienced eye recognised. They only came when Ricky was particularly angry or upset. She knew definitely now that she was right. Then he said:

'I think you're mistaken, my dear Amanda. And, anyhow, I don't intend to lure Judy into remaining as your help and comfort, even if I thought I could do so. You are, without doubt, the most unscrupulous person I've ever known in my life!'

With which he turned and walked out of her boudoir.

Mrs. Richard Portal lay back on her cushions and smoked thoughtfully. There was a faint — very faint colour in her cheeks. Ricky's manner as he received her flippant observations upon Judy was final proof to her that her suspicions were correct, and gave her a very great deal to think about for a long time. Suddenly she threw away her cigarette, turned her face to the satin cushion, and began to laugh hysterically. When she finished laughing, there were tears in her eyes. For the brilliant egotist saw herself, perhaps for the first time, not as the beautiful, irresistible Amanda, but as a failure. Somebody who had failed as a wife — as a woman.

Somebody who had tried to make a failure of Ricky, too. Ricky who had had ideals when she married him. But amongst all the rotten, selfish things that she had done, she saw plainly that the most rotten and selfish was to keep him chained to her side because she hadn't the courage to leave him for a man with a lesser income. And because she had secretly hoped that he would find somebody else and give her a divorce and a third of his money.

And now he had found somebody. And that somebody was Judy. It was plain as a pikestaff that he was in love with Judy, and that she was in love with him. But of course Judy would never give way to any such love, and never allow Ricky to give way to it. They were both prepared to suffer and leave her, as usual, receiving everything — giving nothing.

The discovery she had made had been a tremendous shock to her, and at the moment she found it hard to analyse the situation or look at the thing at all clearly. And she decided that she would tell Hugh Martin about it and ask his advice. He was steady and sensible. He could look at the whole business more impersonally than she could. She wouldn't tell him at first who the girl was, she thought, because although Judy had told her that she and Hugh were only friends, she wanted a completely fresh opinion from someone who was not mixed up in the matter.

She picked up the telephone and gave the exchange the doctor's number.

He answered the call himself.

'Hullo.'

'Oh, hullo — is that you, Hugh?'

'Yes, speaking. Is it Amanda?'

'Yes, Amanda, here.'

'Oh hullo. What can I do for you? Leg all right?'

'Quite all right. But listen, Hugh. Can you come round this evening? I want to talk to you about something rather important.'

'Yes, of course I will, my dear. What time?'

'Coffee at eight-thirty. I'll get rid of Judy and Ricky. I want to speak to you alone, especially, doc.'

'Sounds very mysterious,' came from Hugh. 'And did you say Ricky was home? I didn't know you were expecting him so soon as this.'

'Well, as a matter of fact, I wasn't,' said Amanda. 'But he's just arrived, complete with bag and baggage.'

'I see. Well then, expect me at eight-thirty.'

'I will. And thanks awfully. Bye-bye.'

Amanda hung up the receiver, and then, without bothering to ring for Judy to come and help her, she changed into a black dinner dress and went slowly downstairs.

13

'What is it you want to talk to me about, Amanda?'

Ricky's wife and the doctor were sitting alone together in the drawing-room at 'White Monks', drinking coffee and smoking cigarettes. Ricky was up in his room unpacking, and Judy had gone for a stroll.

Hugh had no idea what Amanda wanted to talk to him about, but it struck him that she looked much more preoccupied than usual, and wondered what had happened to make her come to him for advice. Amanda, as a rule, never solicited help from anyone. She did what she liked, and went her own sweet way without worrying about anything.

This serious mood was quite new to Hugh Martin. All the time he had known this patient, he had never seen her quite like this. Something quite out of the ordinary must have happened.

'What is it, my dear?' he asked again.

She drained her coffee cup, put it down on the little table beside her, then gazed at the red point of her cigarette.

'Physician mine,' she said at length, 'I want your advice badly.'

He waited for a moment for her to continue, but she seemed at a loss how to explain herself, so he prompted her.

'What about? You and Traill . . . ? You know I'll help in any way I can.'

'No, not Edward. It's Ricky.'

'Ricky? What's the matter with him? Isn't he fit, Amanda?'

'Yes, there's nothing the matter with him in that way,' she replied. 'In fact, he's looking grand. But I have good reason to believe — in fact I know — that he's fallen in love.'

Hugh glanced at her quickly. Had she found out about Ricky's affair with Judy? If so, how much did she know? It was unlikely that she knew about the episode at the inn. And Hugh wondered whether or not he ought to tell her. After leaving Judy last night he had come to the conclusion that he had behaved like a cad. He had also decided that it was none of his business. But if Amanda knew about the affair, and had called upon him to help her, it might be necessary to tell her.

He decided that he had better wait and see what Amanda had to say first, and pretend to know nothing about the matter until she had told him her story.

After all, it might be something quite different. Ricky had only been home an hour or two. There had not been much time for her to discover that he had been carrying on an affair with her cousin. Perhaps he had met some girl abroad and had fallen in love out there.

'What on earth makes you think Ricky's in love?' he asked.

'I know he is. He's finished with me. I suppose, strictly speaking, we finished with each other months ago. He's in love with another woman.'

'Is Ricky in the habit of having affairs?'

'I didn't say he was having an affair, Hugh. I said he was *in love*. If he was just wallowing in an ordinary 'affair,' I wouldn't mind so much. But he's serious, and doing the chivalrous thing and giving her up for my sake. And I don't want that to happen. I'm not worth it.'

So unusual was that type of humility from Amanda that Dr. Martin was astonished. He was a little puzzled, too. After all, the picture Amanda drew of Ricky, giving up the woman he loved because he was married, didn't quite fit in with a Ricky who carried on an affair with his wife's cousin in his own house.

'Well, my dear,' he said, 'what do you propose to do about it?'

'That's where I want your help. What do you think I *ought* to do?'

'Well, if he tells you he's ready to stop seeing this girl, I don't see what you can do.'

'You don't understand, Hugh,' Amanda broke in. 'He hasn't *told* me anything.

He doesn't realise that I know about this affair, and I don't think he means to tell me.'

'Then how do you know about it?'

'Oh, he's given himself away in lots of little ways without meaning to. I know Ricky, and it's as clear as daylight to me.'

'Well, my dear, assuming you're right, I don't quite see how I can help you,' said Hugh.

'But you can,' said Amanda. 'As a matter of fact, I have got an idea up my sleeve, and I want to know what you think of it.'

'Well, let me hear what it is, and I'll try to give you good advice.'

Amanda considered for a moment before she spoke.

'You realise, Hugh,' she said at length, 'that the fact of Ricky's falling in love with another woman doesn't affect me, personally. I mean — he hasn't delivered a shattering deathblow, or anything like that. It's his being so unselfish and self-effacing about it that rather puts me to shame. I don't know how to act for the best.'

'What's on your mind, my dear?'

'Well, you know that Edward Traill and I have been seeing a good deal of each other lately. You know, as everybody must know, that I'm crazy about him. He asked me months ago if I'd go away with him and let Ricky divorce me, but I couldn't quite make up my mind. If Ricky had thrown the 'jealous husband' act and turned Eddy out of the house, I'd probably have gone off with him. But as it was, Ricky was so accommodating, and made everything too easy. Whenever Eddy came into the house, Ricky just put his nose in the air and walked out, leaving us to it. So I rather let things slide. And also, I don't mind admitting to you that Eddy isn't nearly as well-off as Ricky. I don't mean to say that we'd have to settle down to 'love in a cottage,' or anything like that, But I wouldn't be able to keep up appearances in quite the same way as I do now.'

A half smile played round Hugh's mouth.

'That's pretty honest, at any rate,' he remarked.

'Well, it's true, so why not admit it? Ricky knows that perfectly well, too. That's why I feel such a beast now. I've been carrying on an affair in my own home, regardless of Ricky's feelings, and have practically turned him out of the house on dozens of occasions. Yet when he happens to fall in love with another girl, he not only does the right thing and gives her up on the spot, but he comes back to me and means to go on as before, and say nothing about it. He's made me feel such a selfish little brute. It's not fair on him, is it, Hugh?'

Amanda in this kind of mood was completely baffling to Hugh Martin. He was used to dealing with the selfish, egotistical woman who never paused to consider anyone's point of view but her own, and who went through life getting just what she wanted through her pure physical charm. But he was a little worried by her attitude. If Amanda was suddenly conscience-stricken about Ricky, he felt all the more that he ought to tell her that Portal was not altogether the paragon that she believed.

'Do you want to know whether I think you ought to put an end to the affair with Traill, and settle down with Ricky?' he asked.

For a moment Amanda gazed at him in blank astonishment. Then she gave a little laugh.

'Hugh — *darling*, you've got the wrong end of the stick *completely*. Such a thought never entered my head. No — what I want to know is whether you think I'd be justified in running away with Edward and letting Ricky divorce me.'

Hugh stared back.

'Amanda, you're not thinking of going away with Traill, of landing yourself in for all that scandal!'

'Yes — a good elopement, Hugh. That's such a lovely old-fashioned word. But that's what it comes to, I suppose. I want to elope with Eddy. I was fast making up my mind to do so before our accident. Now Ricky's falling in love has hastened matters up a bit. It gives me an extra reason for going, knowing that it will make things easier for him. I realise I haven't made him happy, Hugh. I'm not the sort of person he ought to have married, anyway. I'm much too restless. Ricky oughtn't to be tied to someone who's always letting him in for shows and parties and entertaining. He's the type to settle down by the fireside and be all domesticated behind a newspaper.'

Hugh could not resist a smile at the picture conjured up by Amanda's flippant remarks. But he wondered whether Amanda would be so sorry for Ricky, or quite so anxious to go away with Traill and leave the field clear for him, if she knew the truth.

'Amanda,' he said, 'you can't honestly mean to run away with Traill like this, in a moment of quixotry, just because you think you've treated Ricky badly, and because you think he wants his freedom in order to marry someone else.'

Amanda made an irritable gesture.

'Hugh, you've got it all wrong. I shouldn't be running away in a moment of quixotry. I'm in love with Edward, and I've been thinking of going away with him for weeks. Knowing Ricky wants to be free has just helped me to make up my mind, that's all.'

'I see,' said Hugh, and thought hard for a moment. And he decided suddenly that he couldn't let Amanda do this thing, thinking her husband was entirely faithful to her. It was his duty to tell her what he knew.

'Who is the girl Ricky is in love with?' he asked suddenly.

Amanda saw no reason for keeping back the name any longer.

'As a matter of fact, Hugh,' she said, 'it's Judy.'

'I thought so,' he said.

Amanda raised her brows.

'Oh, so you guessed, did you? I

thought you'd be surprised. But you *couldn't* have known.'

'On the contrary, I have known all the time,' he told her. 'I've known about it for months.'

'But how — I don't understand — how?'

'My dear,' he said, 'perhaps you didn't know that the affair between Judy and Ricky started before she ever came to 'White Monks'.'

Amanda was thoroughly startled.

'But, Hugh, it *couldn't*. They didn't know each other. What do you mean?'

'Just this. I feel it my duty to let you know that I saw them together the night before Judy came here, at an inn at Checkley. And I know they had booked for the night. Whether they spent it together or not, I don't know.'

Amanda was aghast.

'Hugh! What are you saying — Judy and Ricky spent a night at Checkley together! It's impossible! What on earth makes you say such a thing?'

Hugh told her briefly what he knew

of the events of that evening. When he had finished, Amanda sat very still. She was white with anger.

'How *could* she come here after that? How dared she? Pretending she'd never met Ricky before! I'd never have believed it of them. And I thought they were being so honourable, so decent! God; why didn't you tell me before?'

'I didn't want to make trouble, my dear. Professional honour and all that. But when you began to talk about running away, and letting Ricky divorce *you*, I thought you'd better know. You might find the evidence to enable you to divorce *him*, and cite Judy as co-respondent. It would at least give you a third of his income.'

'And I was thinking of running away and leaving the way clear for *them*!' said Amanda with a short laugh. 'What a fool I've been!'

'Well, what are you going to do now?'

'Have it out with them. Tell them exactly what I think. They can't do that sort of thing to me and get away with it!'

There came the sound of the front door shutting.

Amanda stood up, her slender body was shaking.

'Go and see if that's Judy. And if it is, tell her I want to see her in here. Then get hold of Ellis and ask him to send Ricky down here too You'd better not stay, Hugh. There's going to be a hell of a row.'

Hugh Martin was only too thankful to do as she asked. He had no wish to be mixed up in a scene such as this one promised to be. He was a bit ashamed of himself for giving the fellow away. But he asked for it! He said good-bye to Amanda, waylaid Judy in the hall and gave her the message.

'Mrs. Portal wants to see you in the drawing room, Judy.'

Judy stopped and looked at him coldly when he spoke to her. She was looking very pretty, with a good colour after the exercise. But her face was unsmiling. She had seen him emerge from the drawing room. She wondered what he had been saying to Amanda. She thanked him for the message, then went upstairs to take off her coat, while Hugh rang for Ellis and delivered the summons for Ricky. After which he hastily took his departure from 'White Monks', feeling that if Amanda left, he was unlikely to continue being called to give advice in that particular house!

14

Judy was the first in the drawing room for that interview. She faced Amanda with some trepidation, although she had not the least idea what had been said between Amanda and Hugh Martin. She was to learn soon enough that Hugh had done his work thoroughly. From pure vindictiveness, because she had refused to fool round with him, he had given her and Ricky away.

There was none of the customary friendliness on Amanda's lovely face when she looked at her young cousin. She lay on the sofa, leaning on an elbow, one white hand supporting her cheek in Récamier style, and sneered — that was the only word to describe the expression on her red lips — it was a sneer with which she greeted Judy.

'I congratulate you, my dear angelic child,' she said. 'I feel I can sing to you my favourite dance tune: '*When did you leave heaven, why did they let you go?*''

Judy blushed. She loathed sarcasm in any guise. She stood looking down at Amanda, and answered with some impatience:

'What's all this about?'

Amanda shook her head.

'Darling, how well you and Ricky have disguised your deep passion for one another. It was truly divine of you. On the other hand, you have both carried things a shade too far. First posing as superior beings, making poor little me feel decidedly inferior because I had a human penchant for Eddy, you pursued a hypocritical course! I don't think much of either of you. In fact, I despise you!'

That made Judy's heart jolt unpleasantly. She changed from crimson to white.

'*Amanda!*'

Amanda sat up. Her own cheeks were flushed with anger.

226

'I'd never have known it except that Hugh saw you and felt it his duty to tell me.'

'To tell you what?'

'That I need not be divorced and disgraced just because I love Eddy, and in order to cover the fact that you and my husband spent the night together at Checkley, the very night before you came to 'White Monks'. God! I'd never have believed it of either of you.'

Speechlessly Judy looked at her cousin. Her heart was racing violently now. Her feelings were violent. She could have killed that man Martin. It was monstrous of him. To be so malicious! To say such things — to make such trouble. How could anybody do such things in all conscience!

She tried to speak, but no words came. For the moment she was baffled. That crude accusation flung at her by Amanda momentarily robbed her of the power to argue or protest.

Then she heard a voice behind her.

Ricky's voice. Low, ice-cold, indicative of the fact that the speaker was very well controlled.

'Very interesting, very interesting, my dear Mandy. So Judy and I spent the night together at Checkley, did we?'

Amanda turned to her husband. He carried a half-smoked cigar in one hand and an evening paper in the other. Judy looked at him, too, and thought how cool and composed he was. But she could see that what he had heard had by no means left him unmoved. There were two ominous white lines on either side of his well-shaped mouth.

'Well — can you deny it?' Amanda flung at him.

'That Judy and I spent the night together? Definitely! It's a particularly crude suggestion. But since it has been made — I shall answer it. Definitely no.'

'I don't believe you,' said Amanda. 'Hugh Martin saw you — saw you both. You booked at Checkley Inn, your names are there — you can't get away from it — and you can't deny that he saw you there that night.'

'Amanda, listen . . . ' began Judy.

'No, my dear,' broke in Ricky, 'let me deal with this. I'm sorry you've been let in for anything so offensive. But my charming wife appears to have got hold of a very ugly story from an exceedingly offensive fellow, if I may say so. Martin, eh! Well — I have a great respect for the medical profession in general, and I have one or two grand friends who are doctors. But Martin is just about the lowest creature that ever crawled. I never liked him from the first day that he was called in. But he had youth and good looks, and I suppose that was enough for Amanda.'

'You can't try to turn the tables on me. What you think of me doesn't matter. It's what I'm thinking of you — and Judy,' said Amanda hotly.

Judy set her lips. She longed to speak, but Ricky had come forward and seated himself on the side of an armchair, at the foot of the sofa on which his wife was lying. He took a puff at his cigar and flung his head backwards, while he let the smoke curl from his lips. He looked furiously angry. His temper was, however, still under control.

'Now, my dear,' he said, 'would you mind telling me exactly what Martin told you?'

'Very well. Hugh was called to Checkley that night to see his cousin's child who had had an accident. His cousin happens to run that particular hotel. Just as he was leaving, he saw you and Judy. He even saw Judy in your arms! Naturally he was shocked and horrified for my sake.'

'Naturally!' said Ricky with sarcasm.

'He asked his cousin a few questions,' continued Amanda, 'and was told that you had both taken rooms there for the night. That's enough, isn't it? When Judy came here, she already knew you, although she pretended she didn't. In fact, you were lovers and . . . '

'We were not, and I pretended not to know Ricky because I thought it best,' broke in Judy. 'It was *not* because I wanted to keep it from you, Mandy.'

'Just let us get this quite clear,' said Ricky. 'Do you really imagine that Judy and I stayed at the hotel that night — as lovers?'

Amanda's long lashes flickered. She avoided Ricky's penetrating gaze.

'Why shouldn't I imagine it? It's the obvious conclusion that Hugh drew — that the manager drew — and . . . '

'I think not,' interrupted Ricky. 'It is merely an obvious way out for you and Eddy Traill to pin something on me, in order that you should get that nice bit of alimony which would be so very useful to you, my dear.'

That stung Amanda. She shrank back as though he had hit her across the face.

Judy, agonised, came forward.

'Oh, don't let's discuss things like this. It's so horrible! Mandy, listen! You must! You know quite well that Hugh Martin only told you this tale because he was angry with me for not saying 'yes' when he wanted me to.'

'Ah!' said Ricky under his breath. 'Is *that* how the land lies? What a pity the day has passed when one could go out and challenge one's fellow-creature to a duel! I'd like a bit of nice fencing with that good-looking physician of yours, Amanda.'

'Listen, Mandy,' repeated Judy, filled with the intense desire to put things right once and for all, 'will you let me tell you the truth?'

Amanda shrugged her graceful shoulders.

'How shall I know it's the truth? Up till now I've thought you a grand person, Judy. I've even wished I could be like you. As Americans would say, I felt you were 'swell', and when I began to realise that you were in love with Ricky, I was sorry for you, and I even decided that it was up to me to get out and leave the path clear for you and Ricky. That's what I might have done if I hadn't been told about that night at Checkley. But now I see that you and

232

Ricky have been playing a double game, and you can't either of you deny it.'

'Look here,' said Ricky, 'you don't seem inclined to listen to Judy, so you'd better take this from me. There has been no double game. We didn't tell you about that night because we both realised that it would make trouble where there was none. Your present attitude proves that we were justified in what we did. If you'd been the sort of person to see and accept the truth, I would have advised Judy to tell you straight away about Checkley. But you, and the set you move in, are so incapable of seeing or accepting truths, that I knew you'd put the worst construction on the thing — if only to suit your own books. But I'm not going to stand for it, Amanda. I've stood quite enough from you for a very long time — too long!'

Amanda looked back at her husband. The fences were down between them now. They were face to face as they had never been in their lives before. And however much her vanity was piqued by his obvious contempt for her, there was a queer sick little feeling of shame inside her that she should have come to this — that she should have lived to hear him say such things.

Once he had adored her. Yes, there had been a time when Ricky had put her way up on a pedestal, and worshipped. It wasn't too good to feel how badly she had crashed.

Already she was wavering in her belief that there had been anything wrong between these two. After all, she knew Ricky pretty well. He was not, he never had been, a liar. And Judy — it didn't seem possible that Judy could be a double-crossing little rotter of the kind implied by Hugh. But Amanda made a feeble effort to carry on with the battle and justify herself.

She said:

'I don't see why you should be cursing me. You've got to explain away a great deal, about that night at Checkley.'

Judy felt her knees trembling beneath her. She sat down, helplessly, and put her face in her hands. Ricky gave a brief glance at that bowed, curly head, and a look of passionate tenderness replaced the cold fury in his eyes. Poor little Judy! Poor sweet! What a shame to subject her to such undeserved humiliation. He tried not to be too angry with Amanda. Really it was that vile fellow, Martin, who had done the damage and put the idea into her head.

'Now, Amanda, listen,' he said. 'This is the genuine story. You know I was on my way from Scotland that day. Well, I ran into Judy on the road. 'Muggins'' — his voice softened at the mere name — 'had broken down. Judy was on her way to you. I gave her a lift, and as it was a hell of a bad night, we stopped at the Checkley Inn. I persuaded Judy to stay on because the weather was so filthy. I was dog-tired and I decided to stay there myself. If you want any evidence about that, you can get it from the garage where Judy's car was repaired.'

Amanda averted her gaze.

'I dare say that part of the story is quite true. You must have met somewhere. I know you didn't know each other before. But what about Hugh seeing Judy in your arms?'

Again Ricky's eyes wandered to Judy. And now her head was raised. Her eyes looked back into his, proudly, without shame. He felt a curious thrill at the sight of that expression on her small brave face. Thank God, she wasn't ashamed of having been in his arms. And he felt that she was one with him when he admitted that particular truth.

'I dare say Martin did see Judy in my arms. The fact is — Judy and I fell in love with each other at first sight. But once I realised it, I left the hotel. Judy went to bed, and I drove straight away to Town. If you take the trouble to question the people at the hotel, they will bear out that statement. But if I were you, Amanda, I'd take a man's word when it's given — I haven't lied

236

gratuitously to you yet, have I?'

Amanda lifted the glass lid of a cigarette-box on the table beside her, let it fall with a clatter, and put a cigarette between her red lips, almost angrily.

'No, you haven't,' she said in a grudging voice.

'Well, then, perhaps you'll believe what I'm telling you.'

'Then you contend that you didn't stay that night with her.'

'I did not.'

'And having found out this great love at first sight — why didn't Judy tell me about it the moment she arrived.'

Then Judy spoke for herself:

'Because I didn't know who Ricky was, Mandy. Had I known, I assure you I would never have come to 'White Monks'. But he didn't tell me his name. I thought of him as — Dickon — which was the one name he did give me. It never entered my head that he was Ricky Portal. It was a complete bombshell to me, when he turned up here, and I realised that he was your husband.'

'After which,' continued Ricky, 'Judy did her best to get away again. You know that. She's done nothing for weeks but tell you she wanted to go.'

'Exactly,' said Judy, 'and when I was definitely going, you had your accident. You begged me to stay on, so I stayed.'

Amanda was silent a moment. While she smoked, her mind worked feverishly. After a pause she said:

'So you ask me to believe that there has been nothing between you two all the time you have been here in this house?'

'Listen, Amanda,' said Ricky. 'Ask yourself that question. Is Judy the sort of girl who would let you down like that. Is she? Won't you be the first to admit that she couldn't do anything shabby if she tried. I'll go so far as to admit to you that I asked her to go away with me and she refused. She said that, no matter how much she cared for me, she wouldn't be the cause of wrecking things between you and me.'

Again there was silence. Then Amanda

jammed her half-smoked cigarette in the ashtray. She looked neither at her husband nor at her cousin. She said in a low voice:

'I don't really know what to believe.'

'Yes, you do,' said Ricky bluntly, 'only you're trying not to admit that what Martin said was monstrously untrue and unfair. Anyhow, if you make up your mind to go through with this and to divorce me in order to make things better financially for yourself, I'll damn well fight the case to the end. I won't have Judy implicated. And that's final!'

Amanda looked straight back at Ricky. And another queer little tremor went through her. Ricky certainly knew the way to love a woman! And this was what she had given up — what she had held so lightly all the years of their marriage. Now she had forfeited it for ever. Handsome, debonair, attractive Ricky, who had always been such an excellent companion, was in love with this quiet mouse of a girl who was her cousin. Wanted to 'settle down' with her. How incredible! And she, Amanda, was pledged to Eddy.

Taking everything into consideration, Eddy didn't begin to be the man that Ricky was, and yet he was more *her* man. He understood her. And he was utterly her slave. But of course he hadn't much money — at least, not as much as she wanted. And as Hugh had just been saying, if the divorce could be on her side, it would certainly be to her advantage.

On the other hand, deep in the heart of her Amanda knew that both Ricky and Judy were telling her the truth. They hadn't spent that night together. Judy couldn't have done that and played the game of pretence here afterwards.

Amanda was unprepared for the next move. It came from Judy. The 'little brown mouse' rose to her feet and went to Ricky's side. He, too, was astonished when Judy showed what she really felt about this affair.

She put out her hand and took

Ricky's in hers. Head flung back, she looked down at the other girl, who was lying there on the couch, brooding.

'I've got something to say about the divorce, if there's going to be one,' she exclaimed. 'When I refused to run away with Ricky, Amanda, it was because I didn't believe in divorce. I didn't think it right or decent to break up a marriage. Now I see that I haven't broken it up. It was broken long before I came. And if Ricky loves and wants me, I'm prepared to stand by his side. I don't want him to fight the case. If you're mean enough to bring it against him — then you can bring me into it with him. He needn't defend it. I don't want him to. All I ask is to stay with him for the rest of my life, and I don't care how it's arranged!'

That was the great moment of Ricky Portal's life. He pitched his cigar into the fireplace, and put an arm right round Judy, drawing her close to him.

'God! that's wonderful of you! You're a grand girl, Judy! And if you feel like that, then nothing shall prevent you from staying with me for the rest of your life, my sweet. Let Amanda get on with her nasty little divorce. I won't bother to defend it. I don't want to. Come on, darling, pack your things and we'll go right away, and present my loving and believing wife with the evidence which she won't be able to get at Checkley.'

'Wait a minute . . . ' began Amanda.

'Not a second,' cut in Ricky, 'we've wasted far too much time already. Judy is teaching me exactly how loyal a woman can be. It's a sweeter lesson for a man to learn than the one you've tried to teach me, Amanda. Tell Traill I wish you both luck of the righteous position in which you'll find yourselves. And if the mud's got to be flung over Judy, at least I — and you — will know that it will be spattering a dead-white page. Good-bye, Amanda.'

With an arm still around Judy, Ricky walked from the room.

Amanda sat alone, breathing hard,

gazing after them. Her lower lip was quivering. Her whole body shook. She began to laugh and then to cry. Flinging herself back on the cushions, she hid her face on her curved arm, and wept tempestuously, as she had never wept before in her pampered, selfish life.

Outside in the hall, Ricky stopped to look at Judy.

'Quite sure you're ready to brave it with me, sweet?'

She lifted shining eyes to his.

'Quite sure, Dickon.'

'I love you with all my heart,' he said. 'You know how much I love you.'

'You've proved that tonight, if not before.'

'It doesn't seem to matter about the divorce any more. I just want to be with you.'

They held each other's gaze for a minute. The warm colour swept her face and throat. And suddenly their lips met in a rapturous kiss. A kiss that left neither of them any room to doubt as to how much they had hungered for this hour.

It was an embrace interrupted by the untimely appearance of Edward Traill, who, as was his habit, walked unannounced into the house. He had come to have a cigarette and drink with Amanda.

He stopped, astonished at the sight of the lovers, coughed, and would have turned away. But Ricky spoke to him.

'Wait a minute! Congratulate us, my dear Traill — and congratulate yourself. Amanda has raked up some glorious evidence against us, and there's going to be a divorce. You shall console the injured wife, my dear fellow. It will be a grand part for you. You must think up some words of deep compassion for that blameless girl whom Judy and I have wronged so bitterly.'

Edward Traill's round, red face expressed the stupefaction which he felt. He began to splutter:

'What the deuce . . . '

Then Judy interrupted:

'Let's go, Dickon, please.'

'At once, sweet,' he said tenderly. 'I've just unpacked, but it won't take a minute to pack again. You run up and get ready. The sooner we rid 'White Monks' of our contaminating presence, the better.'

Traill, wondering if Portal had gone crazy, vanished into the drawing room. He found Amanda there in tears. On one knee beside the sofa, he lifted her hands to his lips and kissed them repeatedly.

'My darling! What *is* this all about? I met Ricky and your cousin in the hall. Have they gone mad? Or have I? Ricky says that he is going to give you evidence for a divorce.'

Then Amanda sat up, drew her hands away from her lover, and brushed the tears from her face, forgetful of running eyelash-black and smeared rouge; forgetful, for once in her life, of anything connected with herself.

'Well, he's wrong. He's not going to do it. I won't have it! I know Judy has never done a wrong thing in her life. And if I let myself be prejudiced by Hugh Martin and pin this dirt on her — I'll be the world's biggest swine. Ricky thinks I'm bad, but I'm not — you know I'm not! Say I'm not! Say it, Eddy!'

She beat two clenched hands on his chest, the tears still streaming down her disfigured face. All that was best in Edward Traill rose to meet the good in her.

'Of course you're not, my angel. Of course you're not!' he comforted her. 'Mandy, my darling, I can't bear to see you like this. What can I do to make you happy again?'

'Call Ricky back,' she sobbed. 'Call him back, and tell him I'm not bad. Tell Judy that I know she's played fair. Tell them both that we're the rotters, and that the divorce has got to be against us. Tell them, Eddy. I'd rather do the decent thing now and lose all the alimony. *All* of it!'

Edward Traill rose to his feet. He

fingered his moustache a little nervously. He knew his Amanda! He knew her volatile moods, the way she could swing in a few moments from being an angel to a little devil — from being generous to the reverse. This was one of her best moments. And no doubt she would carry out what she said. But it was going to be damned awkward in the future, giving pretty, spoiled Mandy all she needed on *his* income. Damn Ricky Portal and Judy and all their virtues!

Nevertheless, Edward Traill truly loved Amanda, and did not hesitate to do as she requested.

It was a very astonished Ricky who was called back to that room to be told that he must not allow Judy to do what she had so magnificently offered to do this night. There was no need for her to besmirch herself in order to give her cousin evidence for a divorce. Amanda and Edward Traill were leaving 'White Monks' tonight. She owed Ricky that, Amanda said. She owed it to Judy, too.

Ricky looked down at his wife and felt more respect for her than he had felt for many a long day.

'You're doing the right thing, my dear. It didn't matter about me, but it wasn't really fair to Judy.'

Amanda wiped her eyes.

'I know,' she said in a small voice, 'and I know that when the divorce is through and you can go to Judy, you'll be happy. There's nobody in the world like her. I'm darned fond of her myself. And thinking things over, Hugh Martin is an unspeakable cad. I shall ring him up and tell him so before I go.'

That was so like Amanda, that Ricky could not forbear to smile. He said:

'Are you quite sure you want to go, Amanda? You feel you're doing what's best for you in letting Traill take you away?'

'Yes. He understands me.'

Ricky nodded.

'That's all one can ask of anybody — to be really understood. I hope you'll be very happy, my dear.'

She held out a hand, and he took it. For the first time and perhaps the last time husband and wife faced each other, feeling some of that understanding which Ricky considered so necessary for mortal happiness.

Then Ricky added:

'You don't need to worry about the damned alimony. You know I've got more money than Judy and I will ever want. You shall keep your allowance, Mandy. I'll see to that.'

She blushed scarlet.

'That's decent of you, but I'm not really as mercenary as you think.'

He gave a half-smile.

'Yes, you are,' he said humorously.

'Oh well, perhaps I am,' she admitted, and laughed and wept at the same time.

Later, when she was driving away from 'White Monks' with her lover, she said to him:

'Ricky told me I was to keep my allowance. That'll make a difference to us, won't it, Eddy?'

249

Major Traill's spirits rose considerably. It was the best piece of news he had heard for a long time. With a bit of extra money, he might easily make a success of life with his Amanda.

He said:

'I don't think I can allow you to take it, my darling.'

To which Amanda replied:

'Don't be a pompous ass.'

Which was precisely the answer upon which the gallant Major had banked. He continued driving the car towards London, well satisfied.

15

About ten months later, in the early summer of Coronation year, Judy Grant walked into the garage nearest the small flat in Kensington, which was her present home, and prepared to drive 'Muggins' out for the last time.

'Muggins' had been washed and polished last night, and was about as smart as it was possible for a car of such age to be. There was a very definite reason why 'Muggins' should be smart this morning. For this was Judy's wedding day. The proprietor of the garage knew all about that. He had given an extra shine to 'Muggins's' headlamps, and even tied a piece of white heather inside on the dashboard.

Judy had come to the garage alone to fetch 'Muggins.' She had left the aunt who was going to witness her marriage at the flat. She was to be picked up on her way to the Register Office. As Judy threaded her way through the other cars towards 'Muggins', she felt utterly thrilled — just as a girl should feel on the greatest day in her life.

Dickon was waiting for her — that dear beloved Dickon who was her world — and who had created a new world for her. Such a thought was thrill enough for Judy.

She had feared the time would hang heavily between her last good-bye to him and this day. They had both hated the enforced separation — the necessary lapse of time until Dickon's decree had been made absolute. But somehow the months had flown by much quicker than Judy had hoped for.

And yesterday the papers had chronicled the longed-for absolute. The case of '*Portal* v. *Portal and Traill*' was over. Possibly, somewhere in South Africa, which was the place from which Judy had last heard from her cousin, Amanda and her Eddy were getting married, perhaps on this very day.

As Judy took her place at the wheel of 'Muggins', her mind winged back to the last ten months and all that had happened. It all seemed fantastic now — that last dizzy scene with Amanda, one moment accusing her, Judy, of all that was bad, and the next showing an unexpectedly heroic quality, and herself rushing away to shoulder the blame.

Of course, Judy and Dickon had had to part that night. What the staff had thought of the strange behaviour of the inmates of 'White Monks', Judy had never dared imagine. First of all, Amanda and Traill had departed into the night, and then Dickon had taken his Bentley and left 'White Monks' for London. And twenty-four hours later Judy, too, left the country.

Ricky had wanted her to stay at 'White Monks', but she could not face the loneliness of the big house, despite all its luxury. So she had found a temporary secretarial post and managed to take a tiny flat, with the help of her aunt from Wales, who wanted to spend an autumn and winter in London and elected to live with her.

Busy at her job, Judy had not found the days too long. Dickon had felt it better not to stay near her. It would be so difficult, he had said, not to see much of her were he anywhere close at hand. And convention decreed that while he was divorcing Amanda, he must himself be above suspicion.

So he had gone back to Cannes, and from there, daily, Judy had received letters which could not fail to assure her of his love and longing. And weekly great boxes of gorgeous flowers arrived from the South of France, so that Judy's tiny flat was perpetually a fragrant bower and a perpetual source of joy to her.

Three days ago Ricky had returned. He had come straight to the flat, and had been introduced to the aunt, who, despite her dislike of divorces, had to admit that Mr. Portal was an unusually charming young man, and that Judy would not go far wrong in marrying him.

Just for an hour or two Judy had found heaven again in the arms of her lover. Then the last two days had been spent in a wild rush — a special licence was procured — notice given at the Marylebone Register Office — and two Air Line tickets taken for Paris, which was to be the starting-point of a long honeymoon.

Of course Dickon had said:

'I'd really like to tour with you in 'Muggins', sweet, but perhaps it might be wiser to take a plane. But we must never sell 'Muggins.' Never! She remains our mascot and our friend!'

Judy had laughingly agreed. And here she was today, determined to drive herself to her own wedding, in the funny little car instead of the gorgeous Bentley.

The garage proprietor wished Judy luck, and rather touchingly presented her with a small bunch of lilies-of-the-valley. Privately he thought that the bridegroom was a darned lucky fellow. And certainly Judy looked her best this morning in the new 'two-piece' suit, which was of thick, golden brown silk, and with a tiny brown straw hat with yellow flowers under the brim, perched at a becoming angle on her dark curls. A lovely brown fox fur completed the outfit — one of Dickon's many presents. Pearls in her ears and round her throat — from Dickon. And an exquisite diamond and emerald brooch fastening to one shoulder the spray of delicate orchids which he had sent her this morning.

Thus the chic and radiant Judy set out in her shabby little car across the Park, this warm summer's morning, with her aunt beside her. An aunt who let forth a stream of sentimental reminiscences, of Judy's youth; of her parents; and of her first proposal.

'I always wondered whom you would marry in the long run. I must say I never thought it would be a rich man like Richard Portal.'

Judy smiled.

'You can take it from me, dear Aunt,

that, had the said Richard Portal fourpence in the world, I'd still be marrying him.'

The little car was being almost driven to its limit through the Park. It passed the Albert Memorial, passed the barracks towards Hyde Park. Judy's thoughts were not on the car. They were with that very Richard Portal whose wife she was so soon to be. And her heart was singing in her:

'I shall never be parted from him again after this. Was ever any girl in the world as happy as I?'

A gasp from the aunt suddenly roused Judy from her brilliant dreams.

'My dear! Stop! Quickly! Don't you see that policeman is waving to you?'

Judy came back to earth. She jammed her foot down on the brake. 'Muggins' pulled up with a squeak and a groan. An enormously tall policeman advanced, thumbs in his belt, and thrust a head into the car.

'Do you know that the speed limit in the Royal Parks is twenty, Miss, and that you were doing thirty-five?'

Judy sat back, cheeks flushed, a dimple playing at the corner of her mouth.

'Officer, it can't be true! 'Muggins' could never do thirty-five at her fastest.'

''Oo's 'Muggins'?'

'Why, this car.'

The policeman put his tongue in his cheek, and pulled out a notebook.

'H'm. That's as it may be! But you were doing thirty-five, and I must take your name and address.'

Judy's aunt eyed the policeman disapprovingly.

'Motorists have no peace these days, and it's a shame! What's more, you'll make my niece late for her wedding.'

The constable, pencil suspended in hand, looked at the girl at the wheel; at her fresh loveliness and her flowers. A smile relaxed his features.

'Wedding, eh? So that's where you're off to! I'm sure I wish you the best of luck, Miss, and him too.'

'Thank you,' said Judy. 'And now may I go?'

'Sorry. It's my duty to take your name and address.'

'Oh well,' sighed Judy, 'that's a nice thing to happen on my wedding day!'

The policeman grinned.

'Don't suppose your young man will be displeased, Miss, to hear you was speeding to him, so to speak.'

Judy laughed.

'Don't forget once I'm his wife he'll be responsible for my fines.'

'Oh well,' said the constable. 'I don't doubt he'll be glad to pay it, Miss.'

And that was the story which Judy had to tell Ricky when she reached the Register Office, flushed, breathless — and late.

Ricky, brown from the Mediterranean sun, handsome and debonair as ever, in a new grey suit for the occasion with a white carnation in his button-hole, held his bride's hand very tightly and reprimanded her.

'A nice thing to have my wife summoned as soon as she becomes Mrs. Portal! And who'd have thought

'Muggins' could have done it?'

''Muggins' can do anything,' said Judy. 'Bless her little heart, she is really responsible for my meeting you.'

'I adore that car,' said Ricky fervently, 'and long after she ceases to work, she shall be put in a glass case and kept at 'White Monks' as a priceless treasure.'

The Registrar coughed.

'If we might get on with the ceremony now, sir . . . '

Ricky looked into Judy's eyes. A wave of sheer rapture undulated between them.

'Shall we, my sweet?' he whispered.

And she whispered back:

'Darling . . . Yes . . . '

THE END

A FRAGILE SANCTUARY

Roberta Grieve

When Jess Fenton refuses to have her disabled sister locked away, her employer turns them out of their cottage. Wandering the country lanes in search of work, they find unlikely sanctuary at a privately run home for the mentally ill — the very place that Jess had vowed her sister would never enter. As she settles into her new job, Jess finds herself falling in love with the owner of Chalfont Hall, even as she questions his motivation in running such a place.

SHIFTING SANDS

Shelagh Fenton

Ruth's father tells her that he has taken on Paul as a business partner, and whilst being obliged to co-operate with him, Ruth's reaction is to feel a deep distrust for a man she hardly knows. However, she comes to trust him and love him as they work together to track down her cousin Melanie, who has disappeared. Then Paul saves Ruth's life at serious cost to himself . . . just as they finally locate Melanie who is in great danger . . .